Joan Taylor grew up in West Yorkshire, and has always enjoyed writing and telling children's stories. She studied English in Manchester, and went on to teach the subject in schools.

She is particularly fond of Dartmoor, which became her inspiration for this book.

Married with a son and daughter, she now lives in the village of Worsley. 'The Locked Door' is her second published work.

The Locked Door

Joan Taylor

The Locked Door

Nightingale Books

NIGHTINGALE PAPERBACK

© Copyright 2005
Joan Taylor

The right of Joan Taylor to be identified as author of
this work has been asserted by her in accordance with the
Copyright, Designs and Patents Act 1988

All Rights Reserved

No reproduction, copy or transmission of this publication
may be made without written permission.
No paragraph of this publication may be reproduced,
copied or transmitted save with the written permission of the
publisher, or in accordance with the provisions
of the Copyright Act 1956 (as amended).

Any person who does any unauthorised act in relation to
this publication may be liable to criminal
prosecution and civil claims for damage.

A CIP catalogue record for this title is
available from the British Library

ISBN 1 903491 35 5

*Nightingale Books is an imprint of
Pegasus Elliot MacKenzie Publishers Ltd.*
www.pegasuspublishers.com

First Published in 2005

**Nightingale Books
Sheraton House Castle Park
Cambridge England**
Printed & Bound in Great Britain

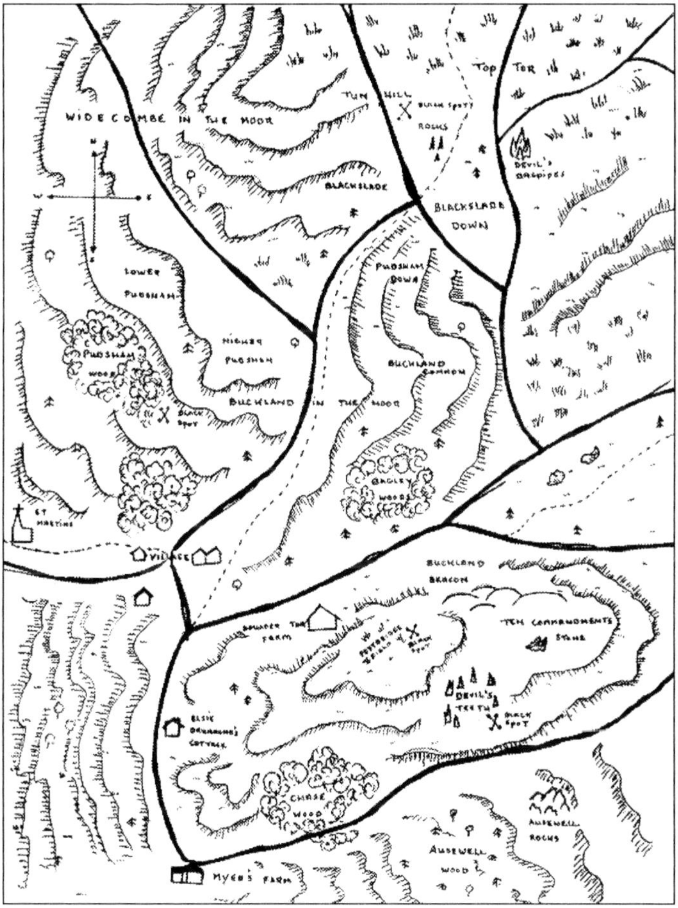

WIDECOMBE IN THE MOOR
N
W
E
S
TUN HILL
BLACK SPOT
ROCKS
TOP TOR
DEVIL'S BAGPIPES
BLACKSLADE
BLACKSLADE DOWN
LOWER PUDSHAM
HIGHER PUDSHAM
PUDSHAM WOOD
BLACK SPOT
PUDSHAM DOWN
BUCKLAND COMMON
BUCKLAND IN THE MOOR
BAGLEY WOOD
ST MARTINS
VILLAGE
BUCKLAND BEACON
TEN COMMANDMENTS STONE
PARTRIDGE FIELD
BLACK SPOT
DEVIL'S TEETH
BLACK SPOT
ELSIE
COTTAGE
CHASE WOOD
AUSEWELL WOOD
AUSEWELL ROCKS
MYER'S FARM

CHAPTERS

1. MRS DRUMMOND	15
2. BAD DREAMS	20
3. THE OLD BLACK KEY	26
4. THE MOTTRAM CURSE	29
5. BILLY'S ROOM	35
6. FIRE IN POSTBRIDGE FIELD	40
7. LOST ON THE MOOR	45
8. GRANDPA'S RESCUE	51
9. DANGER AHEAD	56
10. A CHURCHYARD VISIT	62
11. PUDSHAM WOOD	67
12. THE MIRROR	72
13. THE CAMEO BROOCH	80
14. A PREMONITION	85
15. ISOBEL'S PORTRAIT	91
16 THE DEVIL'S TEETH	96

17. MRS DRUMMOND'S CONFESSION	*103*
18. DARKNESS BEYOND	*110*
19. THROUGH THE DOOR	*116*
20. SAFE AT LAST	*121*

PROLOGUE

'Something was wrong! Terribly wrong. Wide awake, Jessie sprang up. She looked down at her hands. They were blue and numb, just as if she had been playing in the snow. Icy moonlight illuminated the room, flickering across the ceiling and curtains, and replacing the darkness with something far worse – a lifeless silence and the smell of dampness and neglect.
It was no use screaming. She was voiceless. In fact there were no sounds of any kind; only a silent void from which there was no escape.'

The locked door stands at the end of a long dark corridor. Jessie discovers it on her first week at Boulder Tor Farm. When she puts her ear to the door, she hears a funny rhythmic whispering, blurred and indistinct like the sounds from a seashell. The noise makes her uneasy, and she decides to question Gran about the room.

   'Grandpa keeps his memories in there,' Gran replies, with a distant look on her face. 'All locked away, so they don't bother him any more.'

   But Jessie is certain that more than Grandpa's memories lay behind the locked door.

   Soon she learns that Gran and Grandpa have a terrible secret! They are haunted by a devastating family curse, which threatens to destroy them. The Mottram Curse has existed for a hundred years, since the tragic murder of a young boy in Postbridge Field.

   Billy Mottram died a horrifying death there, but what does he want of Jessie? His frightened spirit summons her to the barn, where she encounters a dark insidious presence. Something tells Jessie that Billy desperately needs her help. In doing so, she must engage the formidable power of Elsie Drummond - a white witch whom Grandpa despises.

But why is Grandpa so afraid of Billy?

Each new discovery and revelation draws Jessie further into a dangerous web, in which she must be prepared to confront the stuff of nightmares!

1

MRS DRUMMOND

The August sun was high in the sky as Jessie scrambled out of bed, pulling on her favourite tatty jeans and sweater. Wincing, she tugged the brush through her hair, as she surveyed the scene through her bedroom window. Across the moor was Buckland Common, and everywhere lay the huge rocks from which Boulder Tor Farm derived its name. Gran busily prepared lunch as she hurried downstairs.

Grandpa and farmhand, Joe Blandford stood on the front porch, muddy boots in hand, and engaged in heated exchange. Jessie stopped to listen. It was only about a dilapidated old barn in Postbridge Field, which had been left abandoned for years. Joe insisted that the barn should be demolished immediately and the land put to good use, but Grandpa didn't like the sound of that one bit.

'It's not like I'm a superstitious man,' he snarled, stomping angrily around the kitchen.

Gran laughed to herself. Everyone knew that Grandpa was very superstitious. He hated black cats, refused to walk under ladders, and always stepped over cracks in the pavement.

'Listen here,' he barked at Joe. 'Give that place a real wide berth, and don't go anywhere near it. Are you hearing me?' Grandpa sounded even more irritated. A deep red furrow formed across his forehead.

Joe Blandford frowned, but made no reply.

'Bad luck will only come of it,' he added, by way of explanation. 'There's sense in heeding warnings, and not inviting trouble to your door.'

Gran shrugged uneasily. 'He means the place is haunted,' she replied.

'I didn't say anything of the sort,' Grandpa defended. 'But stay clear of that barn,' he repeated sternly to Jessie. 'The loft is rotted away and might come down on you.'

As she tucked into lunch, Jessie fought an overwhelming temptation to question Grandpa about the ghost, which she felt certain existed in spite of his denials. What in particular drew it to the barn? Had it died a horrible death there? She wondered if it belonged to the Mottram family, who had farmed the moor for generations.

Afterwards she helped Joe round the farm, repairing damaged fencing and replacing broken posts, until Gran called her back inside.

'Remember Mrs Drummond, dear?' she said.

A picture flashed through Jessie's mind. It was of a neatly dressed old lady carrying a walking cane, the handle of which was shaped into a cat's head. She had talked incessantly about the moor, warning her never to stray from the well worn paths.

Gran fussed around, wiping her hands on her apron and placing loaves, iced scones and Madeira cake into an old fashioned basket with blue checked lining.

'Would you take these to Elsie?' she said. She lives a mile down the road at Ivy Cottage. Mind you go straight there, luv.'

The gate was already open. Several brown hens wandered outside, pecking at the spiky grasses. Jessie rounded them up and fastened the chain behind her, before walking briskly down the road. It felt good to be free, with the warm sun on her face. Scores of insects rose in clouds from the blackthorn hedges, which flourished by the roadside.

Although everywhere was hot and sticky, an occasional draft of chilly air crept up from behind and brushed against her legs. The moor, dark and sombre even in summer, stretched for miles in every direction. Like an untamed monster, no one really understood it. Not even Gran and Grandpa.

She walked and walked until the road narrowed considerably, and a rough-stone wall appeared on the bend, covered in pretty blue aubrietia. Behind it stood Elsie Drummond's neat cottage.

As she wandered up the path, Jessie felt a cold chill. 'Something' was staring at her. Her spine tingled. She turned, quickly fixing her attention on the front bay window. Glaring through the leaded pane was a remarkably huge black cat. It was the biggest cat she had ever seen, and its emerald eyes registered Jessie in two orbs of light. Startled, she tried to avert her eyes from the hypnotic gaze; only to find it impossible. Refusing to be intimidated, she held up her head and met the challenge. Then, as she was about to ring the doorbell, a voice called out. Mrs Drummond appeared from the side-gate of the cottage, carrying in her arms freshly cut flowers from the garden. Immediately she recognised Jessie, greeting her with a warm smile.

'I've been expecting you this morning,' she said, turning towards the door. 'Your grandmother phoned to say you'd be coming.'

Jessie felt uneasy. She was still thinking about the strange cat, as she followed Elsie Drummond down the dimly lit corridor, which smelt of lavender mothballs. Inside the cottage was dark and quite old fashioned. Lots of china and brass ornaments were displayed on shelves: the furniture was solid mahogany, with floral chairs and curtains.

The old lady led the way into the kitchen, where Jessie placed the basket on the sturdy carved table.

'Thank you so much', Mrs Drummond said. 'Your grandmother is very kind to me'. She motioned to the big floppy armchair close to the fire. 'Do make yourself comfortable my dear.'

Jessie sank down into the soft worn cushions. Mrs Drummond poured tea from an ornate china teapot, decorated with pink roses. A rich sweet smell hung about the kitchen. She offered fruitcake freshly baked that morning.

Family histories fascinated Elsie Drummond. Scoundrels and villains interested her in particular, and it wasn't long before she was telling some of her favourite stories about rough justice and lynchings.

'Did they hang innocent men?' Jessie asked.

'Oh, yes dear,' Mrs Drummond replied, quickly warming to the subject. 'Many swung on the end of a rope at Princetown jail! They weren't terribly fussy then. After all, if you're dead then you can hardly go protesting your innocence, can you?' She pointed to the bleak oil paintings hung on her wall. 'Princetown is still a sombre place to this very day.'

Jessie examined the paintings closely. They were, every one of them, Dartmoor landscapes and looked so realistic, that you could almost hear the wind howling against the hills.

Elsie Drummond paused for breath. 'It was even worse a century ago,' she added. 'The prison chaplain was as wicked a fellow as you could ever meet. It's still believed he haunts the moor at certain times, but I suspect that's just superstition and games to play at Hallowe'en.'

For a moment everything fell quiet, as the old lady sipped from her teacup. 'How long do you intend to stay at Boulder Tor Farm?' she eventually said.

The sudden change in Mrs Drummond's voice alarmed Jessie.

'I don't really know,' she mumbled, and that was true.

She had no idea when her mother would finish work in New York, but it could be months. It surprised her that they had come at all. The visit rekindled the memory of her father. When she was small, he was killed in a terrible car accident nearby. Afterwards, Jessie's mother refused to go anywhere near Boulder Tor Farm, blaming the place in some irrational way. She never really came to terms with her loss, and was more than happy to put Dartmoor right behind her.

Conscious of the old lady's scrutinizing gaze, Jessie's mouth went dry. Ever since her arrival at the farm she felt as if somebody was constantly watching, only there was usually nobody there.

So why was Elsie Drummond staring now?

The old lady looked pensive.

'Best be gone before winter,' she said unexpectedly,

narrowing her eyes. 'Dartmoor is a dark and miserable then. Liz and Jack should know that,' she scowled. 'No place for a child at all.' Then collecting her plate and tea cup, she shook her head disbelievingly.

Jessie wondered what it really was that her grandparents should know? But it was obvious that Mrs Drummond had no intention of enlightening her. Already she had collected up her knitting in a business-like manner, and switched her conversation to another favourite topic - cats.

'Cats!' she exclaimed, 'Why, I've owned some very special ones in my time. One or two really did have nine lives,' she chuckled.

Jessie listened vaguely as she was told everything about Oscar, Claudia and Jemima; all long deceased, but very real in Mrs Drummond's memory. 'They were lovely Persian pedigrees,' she beamed proudly. Afterwards they walked towards the front door.

'But what about the black cat in your window?'

Elsie Drummond stopped in her tracks, as if struck by a lightning bolt. Her hands trembled, and her mouth fell wide open.

'What cat?' she gasped, the words rattling in her throat. She steadied herself.

'The one in your window,' Jessie repeated. 'It was staring right at me, as I walked up the path.'

There was distinct alarm in Elsie Drummond's voice, which told her something was clearly wrong. 'No, it can't be,' she insisted, trying to convince herself. 'You're mistaken now, that's what it is. You're mistaken.'

'But I know what I saw.' Jessie stopped short, before hurrying down the path. The old lady was visibly upset, and it was best to say no more. She waved from the gate.

'Take care,' Elsie Drummond called after her in a concerned voice. 'And go straight home, now. Straight home, do you hear?'

When she reached the bend in the road, Jessie couldn't resist but look back at the window, where she had seen the black cat. But to her surprise, Mrs Drummond had already drawn the curtains.

2

BAD DREAMS

Next day she woke up tired and bleary eyed. All night long Jessie tossed and turned, and her bedcovers lay in a crumpled heap on the floor. Bit by bit her terrifying dreams came flooding back, but it was the one about the old barn in Postbridge Field which troubled her most. Who was the strange boy she had met? She was certain he was real.

Jessie dreamed, she was walking down a long dark corridor at Boulder Tor Farm. Part of the hallway was familiar, but the rest of it wasn't. Alarmed she quickened her pace. A thin trickle of light came from the farmyard, which was worse than no light at all. It enabled her to see small dark shapes and patches of mottled shadow. She shivered and covered her eyes.

The darkness itself seemed to be following. It whisked through her clothes and hair, as though it had a life of its own. 'Things' were crawling, scuttling and flying after her, and there was no way of escaping them. She looked about helplessly. What did they want? Jessie wondered if she should scream. Gran and Grandpa might hear her and come to her rescue. But it was useless. Only a strangled cry emerged, fear paralysing her throat.

Terrified, she froze. The 'shadowy things' had encircled her. They had funny shapeless forms and holes for eyes. Their thin whining voices sounded in unison, like tuneless violins. They were singing.

The shadows are gathering...
They hide in the darkness,
Where daylight can't find them.
They whisper in corners,
Away from the sun.
Beware of the shadows,
Waiting to trap you
And keep you imprisoned,
Till evil is come!

Jessie shivered as the dreams became even more confused. The 'shadowy things' had vanished, dissolved into hazy mist. A fiery red sun was rising over the hills. She stopped at the edge of a neglected field, waist high in grass and tangled nettles. The name on the gate had two damaged letters; but she could still read - Postbridge Field. In the middle was a dilapidated old barn, with sagging roof and rotting timbers.

Confused she looked down. There, standing by her side was a boy called Billy, who was pleading for her help.

'Are you alright?' Gran asked, next morning when Jessie walked into the kitchen. 'You look so pale.'

Jessie nodded, feeling anything but alright. She had a funny tightness in her stomach, which she always got when something was wrong. Gran seemed tired too, as she sighed wearily and turned her attention to the sheepdog, curled up on the hearth.

'Go find Grandpa,' she ordered; when a noisy screech of tyres and a battered truck-engine sounded from the yard. It groaned and died, like a stricken dinosaur.

Narrowing her eyes, Gran hurried to the window. Grandpa was already outside, chatting jovially to the visitors.

'Humm,' she said, with a hint of suspicion. 'Hank Myers and Fred Goodridge. I wonder what they'll be wanting?' Curiosity getting the better of her, she trotted outside to join them.

Jessie wasted no more time. She dashed to the fridge, and took out pickle and a packet of cheese, ready to prepare a quick sandwich. There was no time to clear up afterwards. Fast as lightning, she packed her rucksack, throwing in crisps and a couple of cans of Coke. She had no idea where to find the forbidden field, or how far away it was from the farm. It would be useless asking Grandpa for directions, recalling his heated argument with Joe Blandford.

But she had to go. Something was spurring her on. It was the face of the boy in her dream. He was desperate and he needed her help. That's why she must find him. Jessie remembered now. He ran ahead of her into the field, and she followed. There was the battered old sign on the gate, which had read Postbridge Field. This time she could picture it inside her head. The barn was calling her. Swinging the rucksack across her shoulders, she slipped out the back way, hesitating for a moment to catch the drift of a conversation.

'Those ewes can't have just walked,' Fred Goodridge said, angrily raising his voice. 'Twelve of 'em, since last week.'

Hank Myers leaned on the fence. 'It don't appear to be random rustlers either,' he replied. 'They know exactly what they're looking for.'

'That's for certain, and it's clear the police ain't doing much,' grumbled Grandpa. 'What we needs is patrols - a kind of farming 'neighbourhood watch' policy, afore they makes us all bankrupts.'

'Sounds like good sense to me,' Hank replied, to a unanimous nod of agreement.

Jessie ran across the rear of the farm towards the gate facing the lane. Turning, she looked about to ensure no one was watching. To her surprise a boy was standing there, as if waiting for her. He bore no resemblance to the boy in her dream. Jessie noticed that he was quite tall for his age, with dark curly hair and a mischievous grin. He was maybe a year older than herself. She might have stopped to chat to him, had she not been in so much of a hurry. The boy stepped forward, almost barring her way.

'I'm Tommy,' he cheekily volunteered, in reply to her questioning glance. 'Hank Myers is my brother. Are you Jess?'

Jessie nodded briefly, but didn't answer, in spite of feeling dreadfully rude. She might have hung about to chat to him, had she not been in so much of a hurry. But company was the last thing she needed at the moment. So off she went, running down the lane as fast as she could, her loose hair flying behind.

'Wait on there,' he called after her, in a surprised tone.

But fixing her eyes ahead, Jessie only ran harder. Her feet slipped on the stony track, and mud soon covered her trainers. This was crazy. She had no idea where she was going, but some inexplicable instinct was guiding her. Excitement coursed through her veins. She felt light headed as she crashed through gorse and undergrowth, now well away from the country lanes. After a while, the way was barely visible, overgrown by dry shrivelled grasses and dead branches. Panting, she stopped for breath.

The fields around had not been tended for years, and an ancient plough lay embedded in the ground. Grass grew long and sour. A fallen tree blocked the way. Jessie scrambled over it, registering the eerie quiet of the place. Before her stood the gate.

It was exactly the same gate she had seen in her dream, with the cracked and frost damaged letters. Even so, the discovery still shocked her. What did it mean? Had she been sleep-walking and hadn't realized? Only there had been no mud on her clothing. For a moment she held back, mesmerised.

Behind the gate tall thistles stood waist high, their heads nodding in the wind. There in the middle of the field stood the haunted barn; the one that Joe suggested should be demolished. That might have been a good idea! It was built of heavy granite rock, with gaping roof and windows staring, like dark accusing eyes. Jessie felt frightened and fascinated at the same time.

The barn rose before her like a monument or tomb, she thought with a shiver. Walls sagged dangerously, as if the earth was sucking them down. The entrance and several windows had been roughly bricked over. Something terrible had occurred here. There was a quiet evil about the place. Cold sweat clung to Jessie's forehead, as she found herself crossing the forbidden field. But she was convinced she would have come anyway, sooner or later.

It wasn't easy scaling the wall, which was covered in

slippery moss. Eventually she hauled herself up on aching arms, and climbed through the window into the musty dampness. Wind hummed through tiny cracks and fissures, making an eerie whistling sound. The barn was unnaturally cold and miserable, with skeletal beams visible and covered in white dust. The floor was stone, solid and cold.

The boy had wanted her to come here - she could feel it; almost sense his presence, willing her on. But it all seemed so unreal. Jessie hesitated. Suddenly, her foot slipped from beneath her, and then down she went with a sickening thud, crunching her ankle on the stone floor. Air rushed in and out of her lungs. She could see her own steaming breath; hear her heartbeat, a dull mechanical throb which thoroughly alarmed her.

Eerie images appeared on walls, and dark patches like blotches of black ink. Something was here; something more than imagination. It was a kind of power, dark and insidious, watching over her, until her chest tightened and her skin crawled. The sharp pain in her ankle was the only real thing. That and the revolting smell of sulphur.

It was all the boy's fault - the boy in her dream. She was certain he was trapped and scared, and had brought her here to show her how it felt. For a moment she hated him.

'Please help me!' Jessie sobbed. Tears welled in her eyes.

Next came the sound of scraping boots and crumbling stone. 'Sure thing,' said a voice from somewhere above. 'Hang on there, I'll be right down.' The words echoed strangely, as a figure climbed towards her.

It was Tommy Myers.

In spite of her overwhelming relief, Jessie cringed. What would he think of her, standing there, shaking and covered in dust?

But Tommy's face registered nothing but concern. He held out his hand and guided her to the least slippery part of the wall, where they were most likely to find a firm foothold. Behind them, the darkness beckoned like soft velvet, warm and inviting. Sensing the danger, Tommy dragged her along, until hardly conscious of her own movements, she must have crawled back out through the window.

Jessie's ankle was deep purple and very swollen. It hurt when she stood on it, but she was too relieved to complain. Outside, a fresh wind blew from the wide open moors, which carried the sweet smell of heather. The darkness had receded. Jessie was just glad to be alive, as she thanked Tommy for her rescue.

'Don't ever go near that barn again,' he said, flashing her a worried look. 'Folks around here keep well away from Postbridge Field!' He flicked the hair from his eyes. There was an edge to his voice, which suggested he might know something about its terrible history.

Jessie decided she liked Tommy, but even so she could make no promises. The field had drawn her like a magnet, and it was impossible to resist its force. She thought again about the pleading boy.

'What really happened, Tommy?' she said. The words came in a sudden rush. She couldn't stop herself. Her voice cracked with emotion. 'A boy was murdered here in this field, wasn't he?'

Tommy faltered, the colour draining from his face. He slowly nodded, and turned towards her. 'Leave it alone, Jess,' he replied. 'That's something your Grandpa won't ever speak of; even though it happened almost a hundred years ago. It's all to do with a family curse,' he confided, 'and things ordinary folks don't believe in.'

But Jessie knew she could never leave it alone. She would have to find the poor boy and help him.

3

THE OLD BLACK KEY

'Elsie Drummond is a witch!' Grandpa exclaimed, as they were eating breakfast next morning.

'Don't be stupid,' Gran hissed, pushing the food round her plate. 'She's just a lonely old widow, who misses her husband. Shame on you, Jack.'

'Well, I reckon she's been telling Jessie some of her silly tales,' Grandpa growled, unrepentant. 'Let's see; isn't the headless horseman her favourite, or is it the phantom stagecoach? Now, don't you go believing such rubbish, Jess, or next thing you'll be imagining devils and werewolves are peering over your shoulder.'

Jessie was puzzled. Mrs Drummond hardly seemed like a wicked witch, but the mystery black cat in the window still intrigued her.

The weather didn't last, and soon the sky turned dark and gloomy. A grey drabness hung about the moor, as if the sun had disappeared forever. The air was close and humid and from Pudsham Down came the first rolling thunder. Grandpa set off to deliver some ewes he had promised. Before he returned it had already begun to rain. Gran and Jessie abandoned the idea of going shopping, and decided to tidy the attic instead. Thunder sounded like a distant threatening growl.

'We best make a start,' Gran said, as she steadied the ladder, carefully balancing it against the hatch.

Once Jessie was up, she blinked through the velvet blackness and imagined all sorts of peculiar shapes. The attic was dusty and dark, apart from a shaft of mottled light from the old torch, which pierced the gloom in a narrow beam. Rain beat down on the roof like galloping horses. The place seemed strangely detached and not belonging to the rest of the house.

'Watch your head!' Gran called, in a breathless voice.

Jessie jumped, startled by the porcelain face of an old doll, which stood out like a beacon in the torchlight. Rolls of musty mildewed carpet, piles of newspapers, boxes of china and tarnished brass candlesticks were piled up everywhere. A fat black spider hung in a web close by, its legs thick as pipe-cleaners.

Gran busied herself, quite undeterred by the mess. 'We'll pile the rubbish over here,' she instructed, pointing to the space beside the hatch. Her voice sounded far away, and drifted in a peculiar sort of way, as though it didn't belong to her.

Shadows deepened. Something scuttled across the floor. Jessie listened to the patter of muffled feet. It was mice of course - what else could it be? She turned her attention to the piles of gnawed rags, conscious of the suffocating smell of damp and neglect. The thunder grew louder. Alarmingly louder. For a split second, lightning illuminated a solid mahogany wardrobe and chest of drawers all covered in dust, thick as a snowdrift. A portrait painted in dark oils, leaned against the wall. It was of a beautiful lady with flame-coloured hair. Jessie felt drawn to her.

'Who was she?' she asked Gran, pointing to the picture.

Her grandmother shrugged, then scowled and shrugged again. 'Isobel Mottram,' she replied after a while, and rather frostily. 'A distant relative of your Grandpa, although he wouldn't thank you for mentioning it.' Her voice fell to a hoarse whisper, as if she feared someone might be listening.

Jessie stopped. Next she heard music - soft music which made her feel drowsy. It was coming from a pile of old newspapers in the corner. It sounded unreal, and maybe the tune was inside her own head, particularly since Gran seemed blissfully unaware of it. Stepping carefully over rusty pram wheels, she walked towards the corner, trying her best to ignore the funny sinking feeling in her stomach. Barely conscious of her own actions, Jessie picked up a stick and began searching through the mouldy heap. There it was; a shiny dark box - with the lid clamped firmly shut.

Why was it playing that tune? Music boxes only worked when you opened them. She remembered her own music box at home; the one with the tiny ballerina. She picked it up, examining it more closely. A key hung from a thread attached to the lid. Jessie's hand trembled, but she couldn't stop herself. She had to open this box, because that's what the box wanted. Jessie heard the blood pumping through the own veins, and felt a moist warmth on her neck.

The lid sprang open.

Next she forced her hand inside the box. Her fingers closed around a hard metal object. It was a key; an old black key, all worn and chipped at the edges. As she put the key in her pocket, something furry and cold as ice brushed across her legs. Jessie gasped, her face ashen against the darkness.

Sensing her fright, Gran rushed over. 'Are you alright?' she said, quickly guiding her back to the ladder. 'Take a couple of deep breaths now. There, that's right.'

The deep breaths didn't help much. Even when they had reached the kitchen, everything swayed before Jessie's eyes. She felt for the key tucked away in her pocket, but decided against telling Gran about it. It was the strangest thing she had ever experienced. Why did this key want to be found?

4

THE MOTTRAM CURSE

Even when she first discovered the locked door, Jessie had felt troubled about it. The feeling was even stronger now.

Maybe she really had found the key - the old black key; all chipped and worn at the edges. Or had the key found her? She recalled that day in the attic with Gran. Yes, the music box had wanted her to open it. Something in the back of her mind warned her not to. But she had given in. The box had got its way, and now the key belonged to her. She kept it safe, wrapped in a handkerchief at the bottom of a drawer.

Once or twice she had been tempted to try it, only at the last moment her nerve failed. The key certainly looked as if it fitted the antique lock of the room, but she couldn't be altogether sure. She hadn't dare turn it. Jessie felt nervous.

She pulled on her sweatshirt and jeans. It was another scorching day. Jessie was puzzled by the sudden change in weather. Joe Blandford described it as freak conditions, after which they were sure to experience a lively Dartmoor storm. It was mid-morning. She hurried Weetabix and toast, as Gran chopped vegetables for dinner.

Gran's hands moved fast as lightning. Grandpa was going off to Newton Abbot Market to buy stock and catch up with the gossip. Then Hank Myers pulled his old sheep truck into the yard, noisily sounding the horn. Jessie strained to see if Tommy was with him; but he wasn't.

'Reckon they'll be gone for a bit,' Gran said, narrowing her eyes. 'And you can bet they'll come back worse for wear.'

But Jessie was daydreaming. She was thinking about Tommy Myers, and wondering if what he said was true. Were Gran and Grandpa really haunted by a family curse? They were certainly hiding something in the locked room. Once or twice Jessie had put her ear to the door and heard a funny rhythmic whispering, blurred and indistinct like the sounds from a seashell. It made her uneasy. Next morning she asked Gran about it.

'Grandpa keeps his memories in there,' Gran replied, with a distant look on her face. 'All locked away, so they don't bother him any more,' she sighed.

But Jessie knew there were more than Grandpa's memories behind the locked door. The best person to ask was Elsie Drummond. She sensed that the old lady was angry with the Mottrams, especially Grandpa. It was time to pay her another visit.

The winding lane seemed to go on for ever, and as she approached the bend near Mrs Drummond's cottage, Jessie was beginning to feel the heat. Although most of the swelling had gone, her ankle still hurt with every step.

The old lady was working in her garden when she approached. Oddly, she didn't look up.

'Can I help you?' Jessie offered

'That's very kind of you,' said Elsie Drummond. 'But as you can see, I'm really busy. My nephew is coming round at six o'clock, so I haven't got time to chat.'

It was obvious that something had happened since her last visit. Jessie guessed that Mrs Drummond had argued with Grandpa, quite recently by the sharp edge to her voice.

'I won't get in your way,' she smiled disarmingly, believing the old lady would think better of it. This proved correct, and eventually she went indoors and returned with a bottle of lemonade and two glasses.

'The garden looks so much better now,' she enthused, 'and you've done wonders with that strawberry bed. I'm sorry I was a bit off hand with you earlier, but your grandfather warned me not to speak to you again.'

Jessie pretended to be surprised. 'But I haven't said anything wrong about you, Mrs Drummond,' she protested.

'I know that now,' she smiled. 'I'm sorry I took it out on you, as I did. Anyway, since when have I allowed Jack Mottram to order me about? It's high time he put his own house in order.'

'What do you mean?' Jessie asked.

But Elsie Drummond was miles away. 'What began in the Mottram family must be finished there,' she sighed to herself; before guiding her towards the garden chairs. 'I had better sit down,' she added breathlessly.

'You mean the curse, don't you?' replied Jessie, before she could prevent herself.

The old lady seemed genuinely surprised. 'So, you know about it then, do you? Well, I never.' Then she drew her chair closer, with the air of a conspirator.

'Do you believe in ghosts?' Jessie whispered. 'I mean lots of people have seen them, haven't they?'

Mrs Drummond smiled. 'I certainly do. But only some are real, I guess, whilst others just exist in people's minds. Take the Mottram ghost for instance.'

Jessie sat bolt upright in her seat, so that Elsie Drummond couldn't help but laugh. 'That's what you really want to hear about, isn't it? I can't say I blame you, because it's quite an interesting tale.'

Jessie listened intently.

'You aren't the first to wonder about Billy, you know. Why, the lad's been around for close to a century now, poor lamb.' The old lady shook her head, as if remembering. 'But I don't suppose you'll rest until you've heard the tale.'

A low wind rustled through the apple tree, and Jessie felt slightly nervous. Mrs Drummond's voice seemed to drift in a funny sort of way.

'A lost soul,' she sighed. 'Why, my grandmother used to tell me that he wandered the moors in all weathers. Sometimes he would sleep in the old barn; the one your grandfather has bricked up now. No good will come of it, I told him.'

'But why did Grandpa do that?' Jessie said. It seemed such

a pointless act when ghosts could pass through solid walls anyway.

Elsie Drummond looked guarded. Her voice fell to a hoarse whisper. 'Jack Mottram's afraid of something,' she replied. 'But it isn't Billy, and if I were you, I wouldn't mention it.' She crossed herself and sat upright.

'Was Billy Mottram murdered?' Jessie asked.

Elsie Drummond registered no surprise. 'Yes, he was,' she replied, drawing a deep breath. There seemed no point in holding back. 'The story tells of a violent feud amongst the Mottrams,' she began. 'They weren't the nicest folks in those days, all apart from the boy. But worst of all was Samuel Mottram - Billy's uncle on his father's side. He was the the evil chaplain of Dartmoor Prison.'

Jessie remembered the painting hung in Mrs Drummond's kitchen, and how she had mentioned the chaplain then.

'A nastier character never walked the earth,' she continued. 'Then, on Christmas Eve, almost a century ago, events finally came to a head. Samuel Mottram vowed a terrible revenge upon his family. Intending to burn down the farm and murder them all, he chanced on Billy across moor. The boy was terrified of his uncle, with good reason. For many miles the monster pursued him on horseback, before trampling him to death in Postbridge Field. The murderer was never brought to justice, and the family claimed that the lad had run away. So that's what happened, and the ghost of the poor boy has wandered ever since. Does that answer your question, Jessie?'

Jessie nodded. A heavy weight settled on her chest. 'Did no one care about Billy? And what about your grandmother, wasn't she suspicious?'

'I believe folks just turned a blind eye,' Mrs Drummond replied. 'They were terrified of the Mottrams. Even nowadays they are still afraid. Some say that Samuel Mottram still haunts the moor, riding a ghost horse lent by the Devil himself.' She gave a wry smile.

'Where was Billy's mother?'

'Isobel,' returned the old lady. 'She was young when she

married Isaac - Billy's father. Apparently he used to beat her and she fled, leaving Billy on his own.'

'Was she beautiful?' Jessie asked, remembering the oil painting of the flame-haired lady in the attic. She was convinced this was Isobel Mottram.

Elsie Drummond shook her head, and her face hardened considerably. 'Remember,' she frowned, 'what is beautiful on the outside might well be rotten within!'

'So you think that Isobel Mottram was evil too?'

'It's hard to say,' she replied with a shrug. 'You see, after Isaac's sudden death, she returned to Boulder Crag Farm - as it was then named. She was much changed. Folks round here were terrified of her. They claimed she was a crazy woman and a witch, and there were some who would have had her burned at the stake, had it been permitted. But it's true she dabbled in magic, believing she could outplay Beelzebub at his own game. That's where she came unstuck, I reckon.'

Jessie thought for a moment. Isobel certainly didn't look evil. 'Maybe she was trying to help Billy,' she suggested.

'Can't see it myself,' Elsie Drummond scoffed. 'I don't think she cared a toss about the child.'

Jessie tried hard to imagine it all. 'What became of her?' she asked.

'No one knows for certain,' the old lady replied frostily. Mrs Drummond's expression had suddenly darkened, as though she was recalling to mind something quite dreadful. 'I'm afraid she just vanished into thin air,' she replied, waving her arms, 'There were those who said the Mottram Curse had claimed her.'

Jessie searched her face for clues. 'So, there really is a Mottram Curse?' she whispered.

'I believe so,' Mrs Drummond frowned, 'and something tells me you might be in danger.' Her eyes stared fixedly ahead. 'Soon the curse will come full-circle,' she muttered, as if to herself. Then stiffly she got to her feet, and hurried back into the cottage. When she returned, she was carrying a small leather box. Inside, was a gold chain and a pendant, which she handed to Jessie.

'Take this, and always wear it, child,' she said.

'But…' Jessie stammered.

'Do as I say. It is a Saint Christopher and has been in my family for generations. Some day I knew I would find a good use for it. Keep it close and don't breathe a word to your grandfather, Elsie Drummond sighed deeply. 'Let this be our secret, Jessie.'

5

BILLY'S ROOM

It was time to act. After visiting Mrs Drummond again, Jessie made up her mind. The more she thought about it, the more she was convinced she had stumbled on the truth at last. Grandpa had locked Billy out! That was the reason he had bricked up the old barn in Postbridge Field, and kept the mysterious locked room. It was also the reason why Elsie Drummond was furious with him.

Grandpa wouldn't listen to anyone. He believed that by locking Billy out, the family curse might be contained. But Grandpa was wrong. By ignoring Billy's plight, he was only making things worse, until as Mrs Drummond said - the curse would come full-circle.

Jessie felt for the old black key in her dressing gown pocket.

Her fingers passed along its chipped edges. It was time to put things right. There was something peculiar about the key. It felt sort of magnetic. That's what frightened her most. Her spine tingled, when she thought about the locked room - Billy's room, and the silent conspiracy surrounding it.

A full moon sailed high above silver-edged clouds, veiling the farmyard in soft translucent light. Jessie peered through her bedroom window, noticing every detail. She slipped into the hallway. Sound seemed to carry tonight. As she tip-toed past her grandparent's room, Grandpa was snoring loudly, and the loud tick tick tick of Gran's alarm clock surprised her.

It was like walking through a dream.

She turned down the long dark corridor, which smelt faintly

of disinfectant. Jessie blinked as something seemed to scuttle before her, fast as lightning. It was nothing; she somehow convinced herself - just a trick of light. Once in front of the forbidden door she hesitated, but only for a moment. The black key in her hand seemed to glide towards the antique lock, as if it had a mind of its own. Then with a quiet click, it opened.

Jessie shivered visibly. There was no turning back. It took a few seconds for her eyes to focus properly. Then, a huge involuntary sigh of relief rose up from her lungs, and she laughed out loud at her own fears.

The room was pretty ordinary. It had a comfortable looking bed in one corner, a modern wardrobe and several chests of drawers, all empty, she discovered. There wasn't a sign of Grandpa's memories in there.

So why did Gran make up the story?

Even so, Jessie was too relieved to be angry, as she threw herself down on the bed. For a while her mind went round in circles. Even though the window was closed, from the big hedge by the gate she could hear the chirp of crickets. Soon she felt drowsy and before long she drifted into a deep, satisfying sleep; only to be woken with a start at midnight!

The grandfather clock in the hallway, struck a deep unfamiliar note.

Something was wrong. Terribly wrong. Wide awake, Jessie sprang up. She looked down at her hands. They were blue and numb, just as if she had been playing in snow. Icy moonlight illuminated the room, flickering across the ceiling and curtains, and replacing the darkness with something far worse - a lifeless silence and the smell of dampness and neglect.

It was no use screaming. She was voiceless. In fact there were no sounds of any kind; only a silent void from which there was no escape.

Horrified she looked .

Fear rose in Jessie's throat. A cat perched on the windowsill; a huge beast, black in colour with staring, lifeless eyes. She had seen it before, in Mrs Drummond's front window. There was no mistake. But what did it want of her? It was watching closely with cold hypnotic glare, and had probably climbed the gnarled old oak tree outside the window.

Jessie's heart missed a beat.

The window was closed. There was no tree outside, she remembered. Only a rotten stump. Yet, there it was, large as life; with thick gnarled roots and twisted branches, as if it had grown for five hundred years.

Below stood the farmyard in eerie silence.

Jessie wondered what could have happened. Somehow, it looked different, even though some of the buildings were still familiar. There was the Long Barn and the cowshed covered in ivy. She spotted several old fashioned gates. These led to the yard, which was cobbled over as in a museum display. In one corner stood an antique plough, alongside wooden carts, most likely drawn by mules or ponies. But how could it be real? Yet she knew it was. The scene was so vivid. Snow glistened on rooftops, wind swept across trees, and only the absolute noiselessness led her to believe that nothing was actually living.

Trembling she turned back to the room.

Down leapt the cat, light as a feather. It purred – silently. The imagined noise sent a shiver down Jessie's spine. Suddenly, the animal darted sideways, and her heart beat like a drum. Eventually it settled into a shadowy recess by a low wooden door.

This didn't make sense. Jessie shook her head in disbelief.

Before her eyes the wallpaper was peeling. In a few minutes Gran's soft primrose decorations were reduced to cracked and dirty plaster. Damp patches had formed all along the ceiling. Horrible yellow-stained curtains hung in the window. She shrank against the wall in chilling certainty.

The room was quickly changing. The light fittings were gone, and the door no longer varnished, was now a sombre grey colour. Jessie had a dreadful feeling that it led to somewhere else, other than the familiar hallway. Before long the floor was empty, apart from piles of rags and rubbish, a shabby table and a forlorn candle; which did nothing to lift the eerie gloom.

The cat watched expectantly.

Worst of all Jessie was trapped. She knew what it was like to be Billy now. How she wished she could flick on the light-switch, and escape the mind numbing silence. It was the worst thing she had ever experienced; that, and being excluded from her own comfortable existence.

Cold crept into her body, slowly at first. It moved up Jessie's arms and legs, gradually taking hold of her mind, until it was difficult to think clearly. She seriously began to wonder if she might freeze to death, as a warm tingle spread through her limbs. The drowsiness had already begun to claim her.

'Gran - Grandpa!' she might have called, but she knew it was hopeless. They would never hear. How could they? Her grandparents were 'years' away. Panic, seemed the only real thing left to her, and an overwhelming desire to escape. She might even have hammered on the dingy coloured door, had the cat not sprang up to prevent it.

For a moment, Jessie stood frozen.

To her horror the door had begun to open. Slowly at first, it revealed a faint bluish light. She noticed the door handle moving, and something grey and cloudy, drifted from underneath. At first it looked like a damp mist, with no solid form. She trained her eyes to the softening gloom, ever conscious of an incredible calm. The candle burned much brighter.

Jessie blinked.

In the flickering light, she could make out the hazy figure of a boy. He looked about ten years old, and was dressed in tattered old clothes. She recognised him straight away. His face was small and pale, so that his blue eyes seemed too large. A mop of blonde hair fell untidily around his collar.

He was the boy in her dream.

'Billy. Billy,' she whispered, but the words froze on her lips and no sound came out. She stretched out her arms towards him.

He looked up and smiled distantly. Disappointed, Jessie had to remind herself that Billy Mottram was a ghost. Occasionally his image began to shimmer and fade, and was in danger of disappearing altogether.

Please don't go, Jessie thought, surprised at herself.

But there was nothing malevolent about Billy Mottram, not even a hint of malice. The boy looked thoroughly lost and afraid. Then the full moon passed behind a cloud, darkening the room. The ghost began to move towards the door again.

'Billy, come back!' Jessie shouted, even though she was aware she had no voice. She would have to communicate through her mind, but now it was too late. The wispy figure was already disappearing. Then he had gone. Behind him the door was closing, as a vile smell of stale bog entered the room.

Jessie felt sick. She had failed Billy, simply because she was too afraid to follow him into the darkness.

6

FIRE IN POSTBRIDGE FIELD

By late on Friday night the weather had grown stormy. Jessie could hear Grandpa pacing about in the kitchen. Normally he was a sound sleeper, but tonight something seemed to be bothering him. She knew it wasn't the high wind whistling around the barns, nor the continuous banging of the shed door. He was used to these. The dogs were barking furiously now, and as she approached the window, Meg let out a frightened howl.

She hurried downstairs and into the kitchen. Grandpa wore his thick waterproof coat, and was carrying a newly loaded shotgun. Jessie thought he looked worried.

'What's wrong?' she said, startling him.

Grandpa jumped. 'It's only an ol' fox, most like,' he replied. 'After the chickens, I expect. Crafty devil - but I won't miss him this time.'

As he walked into the yard armed with torch and gun, Jessie followed close on his heels.

Rain was falling in dismal grey drops. A clammy dampness hung in the air, and there was a vague hint of smoke. The clamour of the frightened animals reached their ears. The frenzied stamping of cattle in the Long Barn and the whinnying of startled ponies on the moor, told Jack Mottram that the intruder was unlikely to be a fox.

'What on earth!' he mouthed, levelling his torch into the paddock. Several frightened sheep had already taken flight through a broken gate. Those remaining were bunched together wide-eyed with terror.

Quickly he secured the gate, before striding off towards the shed with a determined air. Grandpa and Jessie stepped inside. They were met by the smell of newly cleaned tack and straw. In the blaze of torchlight, Jessie could just make out Bess. She was jumping against the wire-mesh of her pen. Another dog called Ross, was hunched in the corner, hackles raised and snarling.

'Steady there,' Grandpa said, sensing their genuine terror.

Slowly he opened the pen door. Bess was first out. Nose down she paced about restlessly, until a low ferocious growl rose in the back of her throat. After several stern commands, Ross appeared, jumpy and reluctant.

'There's nowt out here we can't handle, lass,' he assured her, releasing the catch from his shotgun. 'Go find that fox!' he ordered. 'Quick now, or he'll be gone.'

The dogs hesitated, before roaming across the farmyard, searching for scent and pacing in circles.

All the time Jessie watched Grandpa, who was growing more uneasy. He moved towards the rear lane hoping to find some tracks, but the wet muddy earth revealed nothing. Only the wind complained in a distant voice, or whistled eerily amongst the boulders in Fern Bank Field.

'We'll take a good look up front again.' he said. Bess was even more fretful now. 'What's got into you?' he chided; more to himself than the dog.

The commotion had already quietened down, as he moved tentatively across the yard. The moon cast a mottled shadow, confusing his eyes. But he found nothing else, only an open gate through which the geese had fled. He trudged more purposefully now, shining his torch into the fields on either side. Sheep cowered against the barbed-wire fence, alarmed and watchful. Then calling the dogs to heel, he headed back to the farmhouse with a weary gait.

'Strange night,' he confided to Jessie, securing the bolt behind them. 'Now off up to bed before Gran sees you.' After which he made a mug of strong coffee, and then settled in his rocking chair by the fire.

Outside, a curious red mist had arisen, and the smell of smoke and fire grew stronger.

Early on Sunday morning, Tommy Myers rode his piebald pony into the yard. Jessie surprised herself by feeling really pleased to see him.

'Hi there, Jess,' he called out, sweeping the dark hair from his eyes. 'You didn't get my message then?'

'What message?' she replied. She was wondering what had brought him here so early.

Tommy dismounted, throwing his reins over the gate. 'I phoned your Gran early yesterday,' he added. 'I need to talk to you real bad.'

'Gran forgets things sometimes,' Jessie apologised. 'She'll probably remember next week.'

They both laughed. The two of them made for the wooden bench underneath the sycamore tree. Meg, the sheepdog lay in the shade close by, scratching her ear whilst snapping at flies at the same time. A red hazy sun was shining.

Jessie could have sat there all day. 'What did you want to talk to me about?' she asked, after a while.

He looked her straight in the face, and his words were slow and deliberate. 'Something real weird has happened, Jess,' he said. 'I didn't believe it when Hank told me. I had to see for myself.' He turned over a bent horseshoe in his hand.

'What Tommy?' she replied, sensing his agitation. Her throat felt dry. An awful feeling of dread came over her.

Tommy glanced down at his feet. 'It's the old barn in Postbridge Field,' he sighed. 'On Friday it burnt right down, and is nothing now but a pile of ashes.'

Grandpa walked close by, swinging two buckets.

Tommy lowered his voice, and put his finger to his mouth. 'I don't think your Grandpa knows yet,' he added, 'or if he does, he isn't letting on.'

The colour drained from Jessie's cheek.

If the barn had been destroyed, what would become of Billy? She imagined the boy frantically escaping from his evil uncle. Even though he died in Postbridge Field, she knew the barn was still a kind of refuge for him. It had always had an important place in his life. Didn't Mrs Drummond say he often slept there?

Jessie scrambled to her feet. In spite of the warming sun, an icy cold tingle crept down her neck and a tight knot formed in her stomach. She remembered the strange episode in the farmyard late on Friday night. There had been a distinct burning smell on the wind. Was Postbridge Barn on fire?

Jessie ran as hard as she could. She knew the way along the rugged uneven track, through beds of nettles and stagnant ponds, over a broken old bridge, then into untended fields where not a single sheep grazed. Somehow, it had engrained itself on her memory.

Now the back of her legs ached, and her injured ankle throbbed - reminding her of the first visit!

Soon she found herself at the damaged gate to Postbridge Field. Now a pile of blackened wood, it was hardly recognizable. To her amazement Tommy had arrived before her, obviously knowing a short cut.

'It's kind of odd, isn't it?' he said, surveying the scene of utter devastation. The entire plot had been incinerated and consumed by furnace heat. Nothing of the barn remained, only a pile of ashes, from which small trails of smoke drifted upwards.

'What could have caused the fire?' Jessie said, feeling suddenly calmer, as they wandered through the still warm field. No natural force could have caused this blaze, she thought, especially on a wet and windy night.

'Wait on, Jess,' Tommy called, hurrying after her. Suddenly she turned towards him, her face ashen white.

They stood amongst piles of smouldering ashes, thick as snowdrifts. Occasionally dormant sparks sprang back to life, and an overwhelming smell of burning almost choked them. Tommy showed her the old twisted horseshoe.

'I found it over there,' he said, handing it to her.

Jessie turned it over in her hand. It was definitely antique, with sharp defined edges, probably dating back a hundred years. She looked back at Tommy questioningly.

'Look, there were hoof prints in the field as well,' he frowned. I know it sounds crazy, but they matched this old shoe.

I can't explain it, unless it was some kind of hoax.

Had the ghost of Samuel Mottram ridden through the flaming field? Jessie shivered.

She wondered if he was pursuing Billy.

Tommy stamped his feet. 'I think we should go home now,' he said, poking the melting soles of his trainers. 'This place gives me the creeps.'

'Me too,' Jessie replied, feeling again that someone was watching her.

She glanced over her shoulder uneasily. Everything seemed so still and quiet. There wasn't a sound, apart from the crunching ashes beneath their feet. In her mind she could clearly see the haunted barn, with its odd staring windows and gaping roof. She recalled the insidious presence she felt, when trapped inside. This wasn't supposed to happen. Jessie believed the burning of the barn would unleash some kind of evil. Grandpa had bricked up the entrance, in a futile attempt to contain it.

With a heavy heart, she followed Tommy out of Postbridge Field.

7

LOST ON THE MOOR

As weeks passed the nights grew longer and darker. Dartmoor was gripped by harsh weather, sapping it of life. Jessie noticed that many of the birds had already gone, leaving familiar woodlands still and silent. She was attending the local school, and that kept her busy; but at weekends she roamed across the moor with Tommy, exploring secret places.

Often she thought of Billy. Ever since the burning of Postbridge Field he seemed to have gone from her life. Her worst fear was that his evil uncle had finally caught up with him. The key to the locked room was hidden safely behind her bedroom drawer, where Gran or Grandpa couldn't find it. One day she told herself, she would go back in there. If Billy was around, he might even try to contact her again. But the key stayed hidden, and everything remained peaceful, until one day in early November.

Jessie had been out with Tommy, collecting bonfire wood. It was growing dark and frosty, so they decided to hurry home across Buckland Common. Behind them small dots of light were climbing the hill.

'Look Jessie!' Tommy yelled.

Many more lights were weaving and bobbing. Some of them emerged from the valley, only to disappear again over the crest of Tunhill.

'What do you think they're up to?' he replied, stamping ice cold feet. The wind carried the distant bark of dogs, and froze it eerily.

Jessie reminded herself how cold she was. How supper

would be ready. But it was no use; curiosity got the better of her as usual.

The lights were moving slowly now, fanning across the moor. A cutting wind stung her face as she followed Tommy. He knew the moor better than anyone else, and she struggled to keep pace with his stride. Before long they saw a bright searchlight, ahead on the ridge. Blinded they rubbed their eyes.

Hank Myers, wearing a heavy leather jacket was holding Jasper, the Myers's Great Dane. Jasper was easily the best scent-dog for miles around. Next to him stood farmer Fred Goodridge, who was slowly shaking his head.

'We've got to find him real soon,' said Fred, with a desperate gesture. 'It ain't like ol' Jack Mottram to go disappearing like this.'

Hank coughed, his breath steamy. 'Jack's mare came a-galloping home mid-morning. It took three of 'em to catch her. I reckon the beast took fright and threw him. Liz is out of her mind with worry.'

He must be hurt real bad,' replied Fred, 'otherwise Jack would have struggled to safety by now. He knows the danger of frostbite.'

Hank nodded miserably. 'At best he's laying hurt out there,' he frowned, motioning to the vast expanse of darkness. 'If we don't find him first, the weather will.'

Jessie recognised Sam Chadwick, who was a good friend of Grandpa and sometimes helped out when the farm was busy. Meg was at his heel. The sheepdog seemed nervous and fretful.

A dense blanket of fog was already spreading from Widecombe. Hank knew it was a race against time. It was no place for Jessie and Tommy, since if his worst fears were confirmed; there was a real possibility of discovering Jack Mottram's body. His only chance of survival depended on whether he had been able to find shelter, especially if he was trapped on higher ground. Here, even hardy moor sheep were huddled in shivering flocks. A few hours on the windswept heights was enough to freeze anyone's blood.

'You'd better stay close,' he snapped at Tommy. 'We've

got enough problems as it is tonight.'

Jessie felt a huge lump in her throat, and tears stung her eyes. Everything around seemed to be moving in slow motion. Voices drifted through the fog, eerie and unreal. This wasn't really happening. Grandpa was not trapped out there, at the mercy of the moor. The moor would kill him, like it did her father.

Suddenly she tripped and stumbled, surprised by her own thoughts. But it was true. Her father had lost control of his car, only half a kilometre from Boulder Tor Farm. Her mother described the foggy night, when his car struck a tree at full force. After that, she rarely mentioned him; but the pain had lingered on for years. Only recently was she able to return to the farm.

Confronted by her own doubts and fears, Jessie shivered. She was forced to admit, that her father had never seemed real to her until now. She had only been two years old when he died, and could remember nothing about him. But here, at Boulder Tor Farm he had spent his boyhood. She thought about the framed photographs that Gran and Grandpa kept on the mantelpiece. Her heart sank with guilt. Now Grandpa might be dead too. A strangled sob rose in her throat.

'Don't worry,' Hank said, putting his arm round her, and sounding as encouraging as he could manage. 'We'll do everything we can to find him, Jess. Promise.' Then he motioned to Tommy to keep an eye on her.

But fog quickly surrounded them, closing in like a wet blanket. Before long, they could see no more than a foot in front. Since there wasn't a sign of Jack Mottram, the despondent searchers wearily trudged home.

Jessie didn't sleep a wink that night. She thought about Grandpa and the Mottram Curse, and the burning of Postbridge Barn. She paced round and round her room like a caged animal, struggling to make sense of things. How could she sleep in a nice warm bed, when poor Grandpa was freezing out on the moor?

In the yard the mist was thick and swirling. Wraith-like creatures danced on air, twisting and turning to some grotesque rhythm. Jessie drew closer, pressing her face against the steamy pane. She remembered the 'shadowy things' in her dream, and recognised their movement. It was so fast and fluid that it couldn't have been natural. Yet it fascinated her. The 'shadowy things' had a kind of grace. They gyrated and dissolved; only to reappear again, with distorted heads and long wavering arms. Suddenly those arms were stretching out like tentacles. A cold shudder passed along Jessie's spine. They wanted to pull her through the window and out into the darkness.

'Go away!' she mouthed, switching on her torch. Quick as lightning they were gone, scuttling, crawling and flying into the dark void where they belonged. Jessie sighed, and slumped down on her bed.

Occasionally she heard muffled sobs from Gran's room.

Night lingered on, and daylight never seemed to arrive, until determined to do something, she slipped out into the hallway. There she watched her own shadow, like a thin towering giant, as it passed along the wall towards the locked door. Maybe Billy could help her find Grandpa.

She had put the key in her dressing gown pocket. Quiet as a mouse, Jessie stole towards the forbidden door. She slipped the key in the lock and quickly turned it.

'Billy, you've got to help me,' she whispered. Then something touched her shoulder, and poor Jessie almost jumped out of her skin. She swung round.

It was Gran, who had quietly crept up behind her. 'And do you think he will?' she said.

'What!' Jessie exclaimed, her face pale and blank.

'Billy - help you?' repeated Gran.

Jessie struggled for words. It was so difficult to explain. She was caught red-handed opening the forbidden door. What would Gran think, now she had discovered the truth? A conspiracy of silence surrounded Billy's room, where Grandpa had tried to lock the family curse away.

Suddenly, Mrs Drummond's words came flooding back to her. 'What began in the Mottram family must be finished there'. Now they spoke of terrible danger, and possibly held the key to

Grandpa's disappearance.

Gran looked drained. 'You don't have to make excuses,' she faltered, her eyes puffy with crying. 'I know you've been in here already.'

Jessie swallowed, feeling uncomfortable. 'I thought you'd be furious,' she said, at last.

'No, I'm not mad at you ,' Gran replied, as the two of them walked into Billy's room. She took Jessie's hand. 'I think I've got some explaining to do.'

An icy chill met them and the place was uncomfortably cold.

'A long time ago something really terrible happened at this farm,' Gran began. 'It was so dreadful that the evil has lingered on; passed down through generations. No Mottram could ever rid themselves of that evil. In fact it has grown stronger over the years.'

'I know,' Jessie whispered quietly.

But Gran didn't hear her. Lost in her own world, she continued..

'Your Grandpa was unable to face the truth, you know. Some people are like that. He refused even to discuss it, although it hung over him like a heavy black cloud. Lately, things got worse, especially after Postbridge Barn burnt down.'

Jessie felt a surge of guilt and fear. What if she had something to do with it? She should have followed Grandpa's advice, and stayed away from that barn.

'Like I was saying,' Gran continued, drawing a pained breath, 'he just pretended it didn't matter. That it was no big deal.' She shrugged her shoulders hopelessly. 'I wasn't fooled though. I guessed your Grandpa had some kind of premonition. He was convinced something really bad was about to happen to him. You should have seen his face, Jessie'. Gran choked back a sob. 'Please tell me why you came to Billy's room?' she pleaded.

Jessie faced her. It was no time for secrets. 'I came here to beg for Billy's help,' she admitted.

'Billy's help?' Gran repeated in an incredulous voice,

unable to take it in. 'Doesn't Billy Mottram hate us?'

'Of course not,' Jessie replied. 'Billy only wants you to let him in.'

'Let him in.' Gran sounded amazed.

Jessie nodded. 'There's nothing to be frightened about. Billy wouldn't harm a fly. By locking him out, Grandpa only reinforced the curse. Besides it isn't Billy, Grandpa fears.'

Gran remained quiet for a while as if she was thinking. She played nervously with the frayed edge of her dressing gown. Even now it was difficult to face her ghosts.

Soon dawn arrived, bathing the moor in misty light. Already rescue teams were scaling the hills, like scores of brightly coloured beetles. Jessie pulled on her windcheater and jeans and rushed out to join them, having barely touched her breakfast.

8

GRANDPA'S RESCUE

The terrible weather continued. A miserable damp fog hung over Blackslade Mire. All day long they searched, but the barren moor yielded up no clues. It was as if it had swallowed up Jack Mottram.

The searchers only rested for hot drinks, before continuing their seemingly fruitless task. Many suspected that he was beyond their help already. Even Jessie wondered if her Grandpa was dead, but defiantly she shook her head, as if trying to dislodge the idea. When night was fast approaching, she trudged despondently towards Tunhill Rocks, lost in her own thoughts.

Tommy handed her the big torch, so that he could see her through enveloping darkness. 'Keep close, Jess,' he said.

Desperate to be alone, Jessie switched it off. She hoped that Billy might contact her. Before long she found herself lost, after wandering far from the track.

'Over here, Jessica.' She could hear voices - people were calling her name. Everything suddenly seemed unreal. The voices sounded far away, almost out of earshot, but still audible. Anyway, they were flat and funny, and she didn't recognise any of them.

'Who's there?' she called out, her voice tinged with fear.

A cold shadowy moon appeared through ragged mist. It stared down like a hostile eye. Jessie quickened her pace. She wondered if the 'shadowy things' could hide in mist as well as darkness.

Quickly she swung round. Something was watching her again. Watching her, in a cold and lifeless way. The feeling was familiar. She had experienced it before; on the night that Billy Mottram visited - the night when she had first opened the locked door! She shivered, as freezing cold penetrated her windcheater.

'Billy. Billy!' she gulped.

Jessie screwed up her eyes, but could see nothing at all. Her hand was visibly trembling, as she switched on the torch. Her mouth felt bone dry, and her throat began to tighten, causing breath to come in quick bursts. She stepped back in sudden terror, blinking in disbelief.

In the wide circle of torchlight - something was trapped. Fighting furiously, its writhing body twisted and turned. The shape was large and black. It had blood-red eyes and sharp pointed teeth, and was spitting viciously. As Jessie moved slowly closer, the 'something' suddenly leapt towards her with unsheathed claws; only to be driven back by the outer rim of light.

It was the cat from Billy's bedroom.

She stood still, unable to move an inch. For a moment her limbs were frozen solid, whilst she stared again into the hypnotic eyes. Now she understood. The cat was stuck fast in the circle of light, as sure as in any trap. She must turn off the beam to release it.

Jessie's fingers trembled on the switch. But supposing the cat was angry? She imagined those vicious claws clamped round her neck. There would be nobody around to hear her screams. She closed her eyes and took a deep breath, before switching off the beam. Thick mist encircled her now, blank and disorientating. But to Jessie's surprise, the cat was still there.

Something was clearly wrong. Through the dense fog it looked bigger and clearer now, as if regenerated. It was staring right at Jessie.

'What do you want?' she stammered, unnerved.

The cat's eyes still fixed on her. Jessie felt like a trapped bird. She stood motionless, not daring to move a muscle, until she realized - the animal wanted her to follow. But why should she trust it? There were dangerous bogs around, and secluded places where she would never be found! But then she remembered Grandpa, who still might be alive. Maybe it was offering to search for him. Jessie's heart leapt in hope.

The mist was slowly clearing in milky waves. Cold bit through her clothing, chilling her to the bone. Sometimes she tripped over jagged rocks, causing her to shriek in pain. But the cat only turned emotionlessly and blinked.

Beyond lay a confusion of tors and boulders. Then nothing else but heather, bracken, hillocks and ditches, which stretched for miles. The wind battered round Jessie's ears and mocked her. Creeping fear shot up her spine. The moor was a monster, laughing at her.

Abruptly the cat stopped in its tracks. It stood, stretched out on a narrow ledge, silhouetted against the night sky. It stared back at her with wide eyes. Jessie noticed that the cat's paws weren't actually on the ledge, but raised slightly above.

All of a sudden her heart missed a beat. She looked round desperately. The cat was telling her that Grandpa was near.

A sheep shelter stood in a hollow behind the ridge. It was crouched low against the harsh winter winds. Jessie felt a sudden rush of excitement. Could it be that Grandpa had crawled inside? Even so she steadied herself and moved cautiously, afraid of what she might find. It was the finality that frightened her most, without it there was still hope.

Time stopped for Jessie.

Everything seemed to move in slow motion, whilst she crouched over the frozen body of Jack Mottram, frantically searching for a pulse. There was blood congealed around his mouth and on his forehead. One arm was bent awkwardly against his side. His skin looked oddly blue and transparent, as though he had been immersed in water. But he was still breathing.

'Grandpa,' she whispered in his ear. 'I've come to help you.'

She didn't know whether her grandfather could hear her. He lay as still as a statue. Gently she moved him to his side. Jessie slipped off her own coat and scarf, and wrapped them around him. She knew he needed help quickly. That it was a race against time. Determined, she stooped through the low stone doorway.

Outside the night was chill and heavy. Over the lonely windswept marshes, a bird screeched out in warning. The hairs on the back of Jessie's neck stood on end. She noticed a peculiar smell lingered in the air.

A twig snapped. Something scuttled past her and then seemed to take off in flight. The ground was covered in crawling things. Eyes, like small pricks of light, watched from dark corners. The 'shadowy things' were back.

'Tommy,' Jessie sobbed, trembling with fear. But there was nobody to hear her. Even the cat had gone. It was a battle with fear now. Her own fear. Somehow she had to suppress it; had to stay calm. The gloating evil was closing in. Jessie thought about Postbridge Barn, and held tightly to Elsie Drummond's Saint Christopher.

Distant hoofs were growing louder, as they clattered over ghostly cobbles. The wind was knife-sharp. She slid along a frozen gully, wrenching her ankle. Gritting her teeth Jessie shut her ears against wild laughter; imagining a hundred madmen hidden amongst the rocks. Surprised by her own courage, she plunged through a storm of black hail.

Dust filled her eyes, horrible stinging dust, until she longed to bathe them in clear water. Black shadows flapped about her head like bats. But it was just another trick, she realised, like the choking in her throat and the whistling in her ears. Only fear could catch her out, only terror destroy her. She heard the clinking bit and creaking saddle, and even felt the hot breath of the champing horse on her neck.

Like Billy, she was running before the horseman. Running for her life.

Jessie winced in pain. The ground was electric. Raw agonising burns were quickly forming on the back of her legs. Then she was flung to the ground by an incredible force.

'Go away!' she screamed hysterically, closing her eyes so tightly that they smarted. But there was no escape. A horrible grinning skull peered down through her eyelids.

Desperately she clawed at ice until her fingers bled. She had forgotten that her fear, like that of Billy Mottram, was fuelling the demon.

Every single nerve in her body pulsated. Her very soul was in peril. Jessie screamed inwardly, as sparks flew all around her head. The horrible smell of burning almost choked her.

Cursing venomously, the horseman turned.

Jessie couldn't believe her luck. Samuel Mottram was riding away from her, across a wide circle of stones. The moon shone with incredible brightness, illuminating a cobbled road, which led to a bridge.

Jessie's heart sank.

There on the bridge stood a boy. His figure was misty at first, and surrounded by an arc of white light. In his hand he carried an old fashioned oil lamp. At his feet crouched a big black cat.

Jessie realised that much greater than her own fear, was that of Billy. This had enabled him to draw away his uncle like a magnet. He had saved her life. Wasting no more time, she scrambled to her feet.

Now she must save Grandpa.

9

DANGER AHEAD

It was early afternoon when Jessie opened her eyes. She found herself in an unfamiliar bedroom, which was neat and tidy, and had a low-beamed ceiling and a funny narrow door. Everything seemed distant and hazy. But in spite of her puzzlement, she felt safe and cosy. A varied assortment of antique looking cats lined the windowsill and book-shelves.

Jessie tried to remember why she was here. Where were Gran and Grandpa? Her mind still confused by exhaustion, only drew a blank. She could recall the vague outline of a very peculiar dream. When bit by bit the dream began to materialize, something told her that everything was for real.

Grandpa had been injured in a terrible accident. She remembered being pursued across the moor by the frightful horseman. Try as hard as she could, nothing would dispel his obnoxious image from her mind. She could see him even through closed eyes.

It was Samuel Mottram. Since nobody was expected to survive such an encounter, why was she still alive?

Or was she? Jessie shivered.

Then she remembered Billy. Guilt stabbed at her like a freshly sharpened knife. Billy had been the brave one, and nobody knew that apart from herself. In spite of his terror, he had purposely drawn his uncle away from her. Jessie's mind flashed back to the figure on the bridge. Billy was the one who saved Grandpa's life and her own, but what had anyone ever done for him?

Jessie sighed. Did Billy Mottram escape the horseman in

time?

'I don't see why not,' said Elsie Drummond, who had brought a tray for Jessie's lunch.

Poor Jessie nearly jumped out of her skin. She hadn't realised that she had fallen fast asleep and was talking to herself.

'Don't worry,' Mrs Drummond cheerfully added, 'if I know Billy, he's escaped alright. Why he's been avoiding his uncle for nearly a century now, so he's had plenty of practice, poor lamb.'

His luck is bound to run out, Jessie thought. But she still managed to smile, as she ate the broth that Elsie Drummond had prepared for her.

The old lady began to arrange flowers on the dressing table. Jessie watched her for a while, feeling an overwhelming relief. She was safe in Mrs Drummond's cottage. Grandpa had been lifted by air ambulance to Exeter hospital, and although he had sustained some unpleasant injuries, everyone was expecting him to make a full recovery. Ignoring the stinging pain in her legs, Jessie tried to get up.

Elsie Drummond was miles away, thoroughly immersed in her own troubled thoughts. She believed that Jessie and Jack Mottram were very fortunate to be alive. They both had deep burn marks, which doctors were at a loss to explain. Next time they might not be so lucky. A dreadful episode had occurred on the moor, she guessed, and because of it Jessie was in terrible danger.

Mrs Drummond crossed herself. How could she make Jessie understand? Samuel Mottram thrived and grew on terror. Without it, he was no more than hoofs on a windy night! Unwittingly, Billy was the force keeping him living. The boy's fear of his uncle had remained undiminished for over a century.

On Christmas Eve, which was Jessie's birthday, the Mottram Curse would be concluded. If that was allowed to happen, there would be no hope for Billy, or any of the Mottrams. But how could she stop it?

Jessie's heart missed a beat, when she caught the desperate expression on Mrs Drummond's face.

'Something really terrible happened on the moor, didn't it?'

Mrs Drummond said, in a quiet determined voice. 'You can't fool me, Jessie. I'm too old for that.' She rocked on her heels, looking at that moment like a small hunched bird. 'I expect you don't want to talk about it, but I've got a vague idea anyway,' she said.

Jessie felt uncomfortable. She could see the many lines on Mrs Drummond's strained face, which suddenly seemed to have multiplied themselves.

'Go home, please child,' she pleaded.

Jessie felt genuinely surprised, as she turned towards the old lady. 'I thought you wanted to help Billy?' she said accusingly.

'I said a lot of things,' she whispered breathlessly. 'But now I'm saying go home, whilst you still can.'

Jessie reached out for Mrs Drummond's hand, sensing her upset. 'I'm in danger already,' she replied. 'Nothing can change that.'

Mrs Drummond slowly nodded, lost in thought once more. She wandered around the room, hands stuffed in her flowered apron, trying to estimate how much danger Jessie was actually in. She shook her head hopelessly.

'Christmas Eve is your birthday, and the night that Billy Mottram was murdered, nearly a hundred years ago. I've studied the star charts too.' Then her face clouded, even further.

'The Mottram Curse revolves round Billy,' Jessie resumed, after a while. 'So if we could find a way to lay his soul to rest.'

'Easier said than done,' the old lady groaned. She knew that only a rare combination of circumstances could counteract the wrongs of long ago. Otherwise Billy would have to overcome his own fears, which was highly improbable.

Next day Mrs Drummond seemed more cheerful. She was busily rearranging the paintings on her wall, and adding several new additions to her collection. These were Dartmoor landscapes, much the same as the rest.

'I found them in the attic, or at least my nephew did,' she commented, noticing Jessie's inquisitive glances. 'There were some wonderful sketches, also done by my grandmother, it seems. A great pity I didn't inherit her artistic talent.'

Jessie eagerly searched through the bundle handed to her. 'Did your grandmother draw anything else?'

'Oh, I see what you mean,' replied Elsie Drummond, hiding a glint of amusement. 'I'm afraid there were no portraits, if that's what you're looking for? Only landscapes and churches, it appears.'

'Did she leave anything else?'

'Well, as a matter of fact, she did,' Elsie Drummond beamed. 'A diary - a tattered old thing, apparently written when she was advanced in years. Unfortunately, it has disappeared.'

Jessie sighed. 'But can you still remember anything?'

The old lady sat back in her rocking chair, as if doing her best.

'Let me see,' she pondered. 'It was rather some time ago now. My mother was alive and kept it stored in the sewing-chest beneath the window, before she disposed of it, I assume.'

'Was there any mention of Billy?'

'Yes, I believe so; but I'll come to that in a minute. The diary was meant to warn people, I think. There was a lot of superstitious stuff. It referred to 'black spots' on the moor. These were places where evil was accumulated, and the forces of the 'Dark One' as my grandmother liked to call him, were at their greatest. Here people claimed to hear whispering voices, and see peculiar spectres dancing on the wind.'

Jessie thought about the 'shadowy things' again. 'What exactly were they?' she asked.

Mrs Drummond shrugged. 'They were probably humans, a long time ago,' she replied. 'But I doubt they would remember that now.'

The old lady was wearing a hooded expression, which might have suggested she knew more than she was pretending. She pursed her lips, as if determined to say nothing more

'Is this cottage haunted?' Jessie asked, refusing to let her off so easily.

Mrs Drummond's eyes twinkled. 'Well, yes and no, my dear' came her puzzling reply. 'Some ghosts don't actually 'haunt'- you see. That is to menace and intimidate folks. But if you consider the occasional presence as 'haunting' - then it is.'

Jessie struggled to understand.

'Try to imagine, if a ghost returns to a place where he once felt welcome. He would have a certain amount of goodwill towards his host. I think this was the case with my grandmother and Billy.'

'She actually saw Billy's ghost?'

'There was evidence in her diary to support it, although she never mentioned him entering her cottage,' Mrs Drummond said. 'My grandmother frequently heard tapping on her window, as if from a tree branch. But she knew it was Billy. She claimed he warned her against accidents, and things like that. Once when she was really old and forgetful, she left a fire blazing before retiring to her bed. Only the persistent tapping, which grew louder in urgency, saved her life. Several lighted coals had fallen on the rug, and the carpet by the hearth had burst into flames.'

'Did she say so in her diary?' Jessie inquired.

'Yes,' said Mrs Drummond. 'She wrote of several such incidents. But more importantly, she firmly requested that whosoever inherited her cottage must never exorcise the ghost. My mother laughed at this. I don't believe that Billy ever troubled her. Anyway, she did follow the order. And myself, I've never had a problem with that arrangement. If the boy was to emerge as my guardian angel, then I should be most grateful.'

'Does Billy visit you?' Jessie asked.

'Oh yes, from time to time - more often lately, I believe. I'm certainly not afraid of him and have no cause to be so! He only taps on the kitchen window. Once I think I saw him near the shed. But it was exceptionally dark, and my eyes aren't what they used to be. But he's anguished, Jessie. I can sense such things, you know.'

Jessie felt troubled. 'Somehow, we've got to end the curse and rescue him,' she replied. 'If only Billy could be released from his own fear, then Samuel Mottram could no longer terrorise him.'

Elsie Drummond seemed surprised that Jessie understood.

'But the Mottram Curse is extremely dangerous,' she whispered, in a hoarse dry voice. 'It has already claimed a number of victims. If you get things wrong, then the results would be catastrophic. Why your soul could be in dreadful danger.'

An instinctive feeling told Jessie that her own father had been amongst the victims. That would explain Gran and Grandpa's reluctance to talk about him. The pain was like a wound that never healed. They kept it shut away inside them, much like they had locked out Billy Mottram. Now they would have to face the truth.

Jessie swallowed. 'But if the curse was allowed to draw to its own conclusion, wouldn't the Mottrams be doomed, anyway?'

Mrs Drummond wrung her hands nervously. 'They would indeed,' she sighed. 'But Jessie do be careful. It is a tragedy waiting to happen, and Boulder Tor Farm has seen enough grief already. Please let me know what you intend to do.'

Jessie felt sorry she could not make that promise. Elsie Drummond would have forbidden her to follow Billy through the locked door.

10

A CHURCHYARD VISIT

Three weeks after his accident, Jessie still worried about Grandpa. She watched him as he slept by the fire in his comfortable armchair, Meg curled at his feet. Recently the dog followed him like a shadow, whining and fretting if he moved any distance. His broken shoulder and torn ligaments in his leg troubled him frequently. Most nights he found difficulty in sleeping.

Jack Mottram tossed and turned every night. In his dreams, terror gripped his heart and froze it. Cold fleshless fingers pinched at him, and his worst nightmares became real again. Nor did daylight offer any respite; his thoughts often returning to the moor in a desperate attempt to make sense of events. But he found no answer there. It was evident that Samuel Mottram was out to destroy him, even though he had always denied his existence. That was until that fateful morning on the moor, when he allowed the demon to creep into his innermost thoughts. Mrs Drummond wanted to help, but her efforts had only been met by disapproval. It was to her Jessie ran, after discovering him injured in the sheep shelter. The two of them summoned help quickly. For a moment, Jack Mottram felt a pang of guilt. Now he went about his duties as best he was able, everyone noticing his quick tempers and brooding moods.

'We've got to get the back-up generator fixed,' he informed Joe and Sam Chadwick one dreary morning. 'It's a temperamental old thing, and will need lots of patience.'

Sam seemed puzzled. The generator hadn't worked properly for years; bits were rusty and it needed spare parts.

Why the sudden urgency? he thought.

Gran and Joe Blandford exchanged glances. They knew that bad weather was coming, and Grandpa feared a power cut. Since the accident he was afraid of the dark.

'There's oil lamps in the shed and plenty of candles,' Joe grinned, winding him up. 'It will be right cosy here in an emergency.'

Jack Mottram winced, the skin drawn tight around his mouth. His face looked grey and transparent.

'Like I said,' he snapped, 'give the generator a go. Look sharp about it.'

Jessie wandered off to her room with the intention of finishing some homework, but found it hard to concentrate. It was pouring down again, and water rushed from a blocked gutter in a wide torrent. She rubbed her hands across the steamy window, her eyes eagerly scanning the hedgerows for any sign of Billy's cat. Sometimes it stalked amongst long grass in the field, or crouched in shady places. She suspected that the animal could make itself invisible, accounting for the unexpected panic amongst birds, which she had taken to feeding on the windowsills. But none ever came near the locked room, no matter how she coaxed them. Even flowers withered and died there! Damp patches formed on walls and curtains, and the place was inexplicably cold.

Jessie wondered if Elsie Drummond had been wrong about the horseman. Had he caught up with Billy this time?

Next she took out the sketch that Mrs Drummond had given her. It was of the local church about two kilometres from the village, done by her grandmother all those years ago. Nothing had changed. Sometimes it seemed as though Dartmoor was trapped in a time warp. The Mottram ancestors might be buried there, she decided. Maybe there would be useful information from parish records.

A quick check revealed Gran busy in the kitchen, and Grandpa overseeing Sam and Joe in the outbuildings. Jessie hurried, collecting raincoat, umbrella and boots to face the rain soaked moor ahead. She stuffed note pad and pencil into her pocket, to begin the impulsive adventure. Then she slipped between the barns unnoticed, breathing the saturated air, heavy with gorse and rotting leaves.

Jessie walked along the deep-cut lanes, bordered on either side by coarse tussocks of grass. By the time she reached the village she was soaked to the skin, but at least a lively wind had arisen to dry off her clothing. She passed along the sombre rows of granite-grey houses, eventually beginning the long trudge towards the old stone church on the hill.

For a while she sat on the moss-invaded wall to regain her breath, before wandering along a path that took her through rows of crumbling tombstones, which resembled crooked teeth. Jessie sighed, relieved her father wasn't buried here. Most of the graves seemed quite ancient. Even after she had scraped moss from the inscriptions, they were almost too smooth to read.

All the while the wind hummed in mournful voices, and creaked the branches of the leafless yew. She targeted the oldest looking stones, but without success. There was no sign of a Mottram anywhere. Eventually Jessie followed the path through a broken archway covered in wild rose suckers, until it narrowed and became slippery, overgrown with ferns and blackish moss. Suddenly, she felt excited and nervous at the same time.

Amongst tangled briar and hawthorn stood a monument; a bare oblong stone devoid of all decorations and rising high above the ground. It was fenced by a wide boundary of iron railings. The tomb was set apart from the rest. Numb fear seized Jessie, as she cleared the brambles surrounding it.

She began to shiver now, her damp clothing giving scant protection against the biting wind. Rose thorns stung her legs and pushed her forward, until she mounted two partially concealed steps. The inscription lay on the side of the tomb, almost hidden from view, so that it was impossible to see from where she had been standing. Reluctantly, Jessie edged forward to read the epitaph.

Reverend Samuel Joseph Mottram. 1848 – 1906. Chaplain of Dartmoor Prison.

There was nothing else. No beloved or dearly missed. Jessie

stood transfixed, hardly believing she had stumbled by accident on the grave of Billy's murderer. She was surprised that Mrs Drummond had made no mention of it. But why had they buried him here, so close to the church, after all the terrible things he had done?

Ignoring the icy feeling in her fingers, Jessie rubbed her hands across the stone, sensing she was on the brink of some awful discovery. The grave revealed nothing else, despite the fact that she searched it from top to bottom. Only afterwards did she notice her bleeding leg, which had been cut quite deeply on the railings. The sight of her own spilled blood on the surrounding leaves, unnerved her. Quickly tying a handkerchief round the open wound, Jessie hobbled back down the path.

'Are you alright there?' a cheerful voice called out.

Startled, she turned to see the vicar of Saint Martin's striding purposefully towards her. 'Can I be of some help?'

Jessie was caught off guard. 'Er...yes,' she replied, feeling awkward, and hoping he would not notice her injured leg. 'I came to search for some old graves.' She shot a nervous glance at the tangled archway, through which she had come.

'I see you have already acquainted yourself with our legendary villain,' said the vicar, with a twinkle in his eye. 'I couldn't help but notice you through the vestry window. Hope you didn't hurt yourself too badly.'

'No, I'm fine,' Jessie lied. 'But if he was a villain, then why did they bury him in church ground?'

The vicar laughed at her directness. 'Why indeed! Dartmoor folks were extremely superstitious in those days. It seems they were still afraid of the evil chaplain, even after death. Burying him in holy ground was a kind of insurance; a way of asking God to protect them against evil. They built iron railings round the grave, and these were supposed to keep him safe inside.'

'And did they?' Jessie asked.

'Not if you believe the rumours round here,' the vicar replied, with a wry smile. 'Samuel Mottram is supposed to haunt the moor at dead of night, riding a horse on loan from the Devil himself. But the complete apparition rarely manifests itself, I'm told, except for the dreadful purpose of dragging you off to hell. A shadow is what they claim to see; followed by an appalling smell of sulphur. It's all rather silly,' he chuckled to himself, 'but the locals enjoy a good tale.' Then he held out his hand to Jessie.

'I'm Rev Matthew Short, by the way. And you are...?'

'Jessica Mottram,' Jessie replied, seeing the funny side of things.

Reverend Short's face clouded. 'Oh, I do beg your pardon,' he apologised, realising she was from Boulder Tor Farm. Jack had mentioned something about his granddaughter visiting. Now he had put his foot right in it.

The rest of the visit threw up no more useful information about the evil chaplain. Obviously, the vicar believed he had said too much already. It turned out that Billy's father, Isaac, along with other family members, were buried close to the churchyard wall. Only the graves had become dangerous and had long been taken down. Now all that remained were paving stones, which formed a lichen covered path.

11

PUDSHAM WOOD

Friday night was wild and stormy. Grandpa peered through the windscreen wipers at the endless torrent of rain. His shotgun lay across his knee, and by the strained expression on his face, he was tense and anxious. The wind was high, tossing trees at Tunhill, and driving the wet towards them. In places the deep-cut lanes became perilously narrow, as they headed towards the depths of the moor. Sheep sheltered behind rough stone walls, their eyes reflecting the passing headlights.

'Isn't fit to turn a dog out,' he complained to Hank Myers, driving the truck.

Early that morning Fred Goodridge telephoned, informing them that the rota for the neighbourhood watch had been changed. Grandpa and Hank were next on the list, so that the duty fell to them on this abysmal night. Any rustlers about the moor would be sure to get a good soaking, they joked.

Jessie was glad she had been asked to come along. Even so, she shivered miserably in her thick raincoat, and wondered why the heater wasn't working properly. She held her nose at the smell of wet dog! Bedraggled Bess was snuggled close in the tight space, her fur hanging like limp rags and whining perpetually.

'A godforsaken place,' Grandpa sighed, looking visibly uneasy. Hank wondered if he was recalling his accident. The moor held some sort of terror for him, which he couldn't bring himself to talk about.

The truck was damp and steamy. Hank threw open the door, allowing a rush of cold air inside. Impatiently he turned to chide Bess.

'Whatever has got into that animal?' he snapped.

Jack Mottram shrugged, remembering the incident in the farmyard, where Bess had behaved identically. He never had got to the bottom of what frightened his dogs. Lately, he convinced himself that there was no natural explanation. A malignant power was at work, against which he felt helpless. If only he could be stronger.

Jessie rubbed her hands along Bess's neck, feeling the taut muscles and stiffened spine.

Grandpa turned to the dog. 'Now stop thee fretting,' he ordered, twisting round with a painful scowl. 'It's nowt but the wind, I'm telling yer. Plays funny tunes amongst the rocks over there.' He pointed with a nervous gesture. 'My father used to call them the 'Devil's Bagpipes'.

The wind whistled eerily.

Grandpa had a way with animals, and for a spell the dog seemed temporarily appeased. He wagged his tail and licked Jessie's hand. 'Anyhow, you'd best take him for a scratch about,' he added, when the dog had grown restless again.

She scrambled out of the truck with Bess wet against her legs. The lashing rain reddened her checks.

'Keep tight hold of that lead,' Hank grinned. 'We don't want to go searching no badger setts at this time o'night. You might even bump into some sheep rustlers, if you're really lucky,' he joked.

The moon was high and the sky looked rippled. Jessie gazed at the smooth, shiny rocks, close to Tunhill. Gran once told her that an ancient burial mound was concealed here. Nearby, a holy symbol was fashioned on granite rock to keep evil at bay. She wondered if this was one of the 'black spots' which Elsie Drummond's grandmother had mentioned in her diary.

The moon had slipped behind a wet avalanche of cloud, as Jessie dragged Bess along a grassy verge. Shaking his head, Jack Mottram shone the torch after them.

'Don't go too far,' he called, suddenly aware of the

enveloping blackness, which seemed to have momentarily swallowed his granddaughter. It was like a blanket, so real and thick, he could almost touch it.

'I dunner like the wind myself,' he muttered, listening intently to the curious chanting, which sounded almost human. 'Perhaps the old dog is right.'

When the moon eventually returned, it shone with incredible brightness on a circle of stones, directly in front of Jessie. The rain had ceased, and a still peacefulness hung over the moor, which looked confusingly different. The lane did not progress in a familiar direction. Instead it swept to the left towards Blackslade, nothing more than a cobbled track

Jessie gulped. She was witnessing Dartmoor as it had existed a century earlier. But how could it be? She thought about Billy, and how his room had regressed into the past. But the idea still left her completely baffled.

Suddenly she felt Grandpa's hand upon her shoulder. 'Best be getting back,' he mumbled, a frightened look in his eye. 'Sometimes I swear this moor has a mind of her own.'

Jessie nodded; realising there was no point in questioning him further. Wet and frozen, without even a trace of a rustler, Grandpa and Jessie returned to the Myers's farm with Hank. But somehow, the incident on the moor wouldn't leave her. She had to talk to someone.

Next morning at breakfast, she asked Tommy. 'Do you think it's possible to see things as they were long ago?'

Tommy shrugged. 'I reckon so.'

'But how?' she replied, trying to grasp the idea.

'We don't know everything about time,' he said, thoughtfully. 'We take it for granted that time always moves forward. Supposing it could move backwards or swing between the two! The atmosphere might even record time; and play it back to us under certain conditions.'

Tommy had obviously thought about this. 'What conditions?' she asked.

'Well, some kind of catalyst. Such as lightning or freak storms,' he reflected. The gypsies have all kinds of theories, involving electro-magnetic fields or atmospheric changes.'

Jessie knew that in the past few weeks, gypsies were camped in Pudsham Wood, apparently in a clearing near the road. She remembered Grandpa discussing it. How some of the landowners alerted the authorities, with a view to driving them out. Folks accused them of messing up the place, poaching and allowing dogs to run wild. But the Myers family, who had close relatives amongst the gypsies, always welcomed them.

'Where are we going?' Jessie said, as Tommy nudged her to her feet.

'To Pudsham Wood,' he replied with a grin. You want to know more about Billy Mottram, don't you? Gypsies understand the nature of ghosts better than anyone else,' he added, 'and if you are in danger Jess, they just might be able to help you.'

Jessie followed after Tommy, feeling nervous and reluctant. They crossed the moor by the familiar route, until they turned along a winding muddy track through bare trees. Grey sagging clouds hovered above, with the intention of drenching them. Soon rain was cascading down, so that Pudsham Wood seemed like a long wet tunnel.

Tommy could barely hide his disappointment. There was no sign of the travellers.

'Something isn't right here,' he fumed, kicking up the ground with his trainers. 'They were here a couple of nights ago, I swear it. They must have been off afore first light.' Tommy bent down to inspect the fresh tyre tracks. 'It isn't like them to be frightened off.'

'Look at this?' Jessie observed, curiously.

Around shrubs and bushes were lines of thinly scattered ashes, which were fine and looked like dust. Peculiar signs were etched into tree boles, and others crudely drawn with sticks in mud. Some sort of weird ceremony had taken place, most likely an all night vigil, by the abandoned oil lanterns and candles discarded everywhere. It was clear that the gypsies had been in a desperate hurry to leave.

Jessie noticed the worried expression on Tommy's face. 'What is it?' she asked, feeling a sense of dread.

Tommy grimaced. 'The travellers were trying to protect the woods against evil forces,' he said. 'These are symbols to warn people, or keep evil at bay. The ashes are scattered in wide circles, providing safe areas or escape routes.'

Jessie felt a sudden chill as if they were being watched. 'Do you think they were afraid of something?' she said.

'More than likely,' Tommy replied. 'These folks are real stubborn. I can't see the authorities chasing them off. They would have stood their ground. Something gave them a fright last night, and I don't think we should be hanging around any longer.'

12

THE MIRROR

For the next couple of weeks snow fell relentlessly. It settled in drifts and piled in hollows, obscuring the landscape. The wind was sharp and biting as it whistled through empty spaces, or drove blizzards across the rocks and tors of Dartmoor. Many roads were inaccessible, villages cut off and even power lines threatened. But there was still plenty of work to do at Boulder Tor Farm.

Joe Blandford leaned on his shovel. The icy wind stung his hands and face, in spite of the fact that he was heavily muffled. It was easily the coldest start to December on record, and there were rumours of worse to come. All around snow lay in thick even drifts and every time he cleared the paths around the barns, nightly blizzards undermined his efforts. He stamped his boots to check his feet were still there, but they were so numb and frozen he could barely feel them. Then he moved towards the gate, searching the narrow lane behind the farm for any sign of Sam. The freezing wind whined miserably, as he checked the open fields.

'Where on earth has he got to?' he muttered, noticing the abandoned tractor stranded in crushed, compacted snow, and surrounded by high discoloured drifts on either side.

Beech trees groaned wearily, and the boulders in Fern Bank Field looked like enormous snowmen. Joe could still remember sledging down Buckland Common or skating on the frozen pond, his childish enthusiasm never daunted. Now winter told a different story. It brought severe hardships round the farm, particularly since Jack Mottram's accident. Although he was making a good recovery from his broken shoulder and torn ligaments, it would be some time before he was fit for heavy work again. There were too many jobs and too few hands.

Joe trudged through the snow clogged fields until he caught sight of Sam and Jessie, their bright orange windcheaters standing out from the vast expanse of snowy whiteness. He noticed that some hedges had been forcibly uprooted, and barbed-wire ripped from its post.

'Thought we might drop off some extra feed,' he said, sounding breathless. 'I reckon the sheep will be pretty hungry by now. Tomorrow is likely to be no better, so we'd best get a move on.' He stamped the snow from his boots and rubbed his freezing hands together.

Sam nodded, knowing Joe was right. 'But first take a look at this,' he motioned, leading him to a hollow behind the frozen hawthorn hedges. In the undisturbed snow, a ewe lay stiff and dead, its neck broken. He turned the animal over and continued in a puzzled voice. 'Not a single scratch; a clean break and no messing!' Agitated he looked round, shielding his eyes against the bright glare.

Joe shrugged, not wishing to be drawn.

'Where's the struggle, or the tracks?' Sam persisted. .'No sign of anything round here. The only predators are those that have kept clean away.'

A cold hollow wind moaned along snowdrifts and the sky, grey and dismal, threatened the next heavy fall.

Joe stared back at Sam, his face blank. The clear tracks were their own, deeply embedded in the virgin snow. He shook his head, not wanting to make any assumptions. There had been enough strange talk but about, since Jack Mottram's accident.

'I reckon, blinded by snow the beast fell into a ditch! ' Joe trailed off without conviction.

Sam seemed unconvinced. 'It's not the only one,' he commented grimly. 'There's another three or four over there, by the copse.' He turned, the wind colouring his face. 'Something's had a field day here. Ain't that right, Jessie?'

Jessie nodded, visibly shaken. It didn't add up. But she

could understand Sam's reluctance to talk. What good would it do? Least said the better, she decided. There was enough speculation already. Farmers along the moor had reported similar slaughtered animals. Superstitious talk was rife.

Jessie was glad to return to the farm. The rest of the morning was spent cleaning the yard. Afterwards, she helped load hay bales on the tractor, and fed the restless cattle in the Long Barn, Meg never leaving her side. Eventually everyone returned to the kitchen, where Gran was serving hot soup and rolls.

The following day was even colder. An arctic wind drove down from the hills turning the snow hard and brittle, or freezing it into solid snowdrifts. Birds shivered in hedgerow, foxes remained underground, and the moor stood still and silent, without a trace of life.

Having spent a cold and restless night, Jessie had woken early that morning. A freezing draught rattled the window, as she washed, then dressed in jeans and trainers, before selecting the warmest pullover from her drawer.

Downstairs, Tommy Myers had arrived, fresh faced and breathless after pulling his snowboard uphill. Snowflakes covered him from head to foot, melting into a grey slushy heap on the carpet. Nevertheless, Gran seemed pleased to see him.

'Come inside, she said warmly, staring right over his head. She waved her hand at the path by the hedge. 'Where's your friend gone, Tommy?' A puzzled expression settled on her face.

Tommy seemed surprised. 'What friend, Mrs Mottram? 'There's no one else here, but me.'

Gran looked startled, then embarrassed. 'But I swear I saw someone - over there.' She pointed to the invisible space, and looked so confused that Tommy felt sorry for her.

She could have sworn she saw a boy following behind the snowboard, all the way down the hill. He came right up the path. She was not in the habit of seeing things. The experience thoroughly unnerved her. Something was definitely wrong. Why, she could even describe the old fashioned clothes he was wearing. Gran steadied herself. Was it some kind of prank, she thought, expecting the ellusive visitor to step out at any minute? But there was no sign of him anywhere, only a single set of footprints and snowboard tracks. She closed the door, perplexed.

'Is your Gran alright?' Tommy asked. 'What do you think she saw?'

Jessie, who had witnessed everything, shrugged her shoulders. She suspected that the culprit might be Billy Mottram, although it was difficult to be certain. There had been no footprints. But the truth was, it wouldn't have surprised her. When the first snow had fallen, she discovered small footprints in Postbridge Field, and similar ones leading to the door of the old barn in the farmyard. Oddly, they drew to an abrupt halt. Perturbed by it all, she had asked Joe Blandford what Grandpa stored in the barn, wondering what it had to do with Billy.

Joe had grinned to himself. 'Only loads of rubbish,' he said. 'Farm stuff mostly; old ploughs, tools and stacks of mouldy harness. Things he should've turned out years ago! Although there's some interesting bits amongst it. Your Gran discovered a spinning wheel from well afore industrial times. She reckoned it should go to a museum. I was inclined to agree with her. Best place for the past, I say. But your Grandpa don't listen much to anyone. The pair of 'em argued over it for a couple of days. Then he goes and fits a new lock, and that was that. No one's been in there since - to my knowledge anyway. A real stubborn fellow is your grandpa, when he makes his mind up.'

Jessie had agreed. 'Same with Postbridge Field before it burnt down,' she added.

'Reckon you're right there, lass,' Joe reflected, his face clouding. 'He's afraid of something, is your Grandpa, and there's many round here who don't blame him! If this farm could only speak, it would tell some terrifying old tales. Stories of gruesome murder and betrayal, enough to make your hair stand on end. There's plenty say it's haunted, not that I'm a believer in that stuff myself. When folks have gone, there are only memories left, and you can make of them what you will.'

But Jessie knew it wasn't quite so simple. At Boulder Tor Farm, the past became the present at certain times.

As a result of this conversation, she felt curious ever since. What harm would there be in taking a quick look round? She was sure that Tommy wouldn't mind. Grandpa was sleeping soundly in his chair, as though wild horses wouldn't raise him. Sam and Joe were busily engaged in the fields above the farm.

She and Tommy grabbed their coats and dashed out into the snow.

Large flakes were floating around them. The day was grey and miserable, and a faint ghost-sun hung in the air. The wind was freezing cold, as it whistled through the narrow gap between the barns, but there was no sign of Billy's footprints now. Tommy pulled the hood over his ears. Soon the stinging draught numbed their faces.

Jessie moved determinedly towards the door.

'Reckon your Grandpa will be angry,' Tommy said. He fiddled with the lock, easing it with his penknife.

Grandpa was always angry these days, Jessie thought.

They pushed the creaking door open. Wedged beneath was a tangled pile of straw, as though a rat or other vermin had slept there. Tommy kicked it away, wincing at the smell of animal, stale and musty. He took out his torch, flicking on the switch, until the narrow beam penetrated dark corners, or hovered over piles of rubbish like a searching eye. There were heaps of tack, all mottled and draped in cobwebs; a spinning wheel, a stuffed fox and a rocking chair, worn and dusty.

The fox grinned at Jessie, but it wasn't friendly.

At the furthest end of the barn, was a tall mirror with curved edges and elaborate workings. It looked antique, and had a frame of tarnished brass roses.

She stepped back in surprise. Somehow the mirror had suddenly turned luminous. Jessie's eyes focused on the glass, unwittingly drawn to it like a magnet. Her head was spinning and her eyelids felt heavy. She struggled desperately to look away, but the mirror wouldn't let her! Nothing else seemed to matter now, as in astonishment she peered into the awful depths.

An image began to materialize. A sort of confused shape, as if she was seeing double, only the image was actually two; one face superimposed upon another! Gradually the vision faded, then suddenly grew clear again, until a wrinkled old hag emerged with a hoot of glee.

'Am I not beautiful?' purred the grotesque old woman in the mirror. Bony hands were reaching out. 'I'm Isobel,' declared the twisted mouth.

A silent scream rose and died in Jessie's throat. 'No, you're not!' she gulped. Compelled to gaze into the hypnotic eyes, her nerves tingled and her stomach turned over. Jessie blinked with shock.

The image staring at her looked sorrowful now. It was changing back again. The dried out prune-like skin had become softer. The lifeless hair tinged with a reddish hue. She felt herself moving closer to the bewitched mirror. Was it a trick? The old hag, apparently the stronger of the two, took firm hold again, and tears ran down the glass, causing it to mist and dim.

'Come closer,' hissed the old woman, whilst her victim struggled to disobey. An impatient hiss came from the parched mouth. Jessie was proving awkward. Maybe, she could pull her right into the mirror, imprison her there and feed upon her strength.

'No!' Jessie screamed, fighting for her life.

'Right to the glass, my child. Don't struggle so - won't do any good. It's warm now; see you can touch it. There's nothing to fear - I promise.'

'Don't believe her,' whispered a faint voice.

In spite of her protestations, Jessie's hand reached out to touch the mirror. The surface was pulsating as if alive. A soft fragrance of lavender numbed her senses.

'Come now,' repeated the hag, 'and waste no more time. Look, I've got you now - you can't escape,' she croaked, in a fervour of excitement. 'Isobel couldn't either, although now and then she tried.'

A nasty rattling laugh shook the glass.

'Then you lied! You're not Isobel, Billy's mother,' Jessie mouthed in disgust.

This seemed to amuse the old woman even more. 'I'm what

became of Isobel,' she gloated, 'with a little help. But she still struggles; her spirit isn't totally subdued. She does not altogether approve of me, you know.'

The glass began to rock and shake, as if it was about to explode.

Jessie watched in disbelief.

'Oh, you do have a champion, child,' mocked the wrinkled old face scornfully.

Jessie found herself being forced backwards. Invisible hands were tugging at her.

'I'll teach you,' screamed the hag venomously, genuinely surprised at the strength of her rival. 'We are one - remember?'

'No we're not,' replied the younger Isobel. 'I renounce evil; repent my sins.'

'Do you indeed, but it is too late for that. The Devil releases no prisoners. You are his my dear, and always will be.'

'No, no!' came the tortured reply.

'Now, come help me with the girl. She belongs with us in the mirror. How happy we shall be.'

'Help me, Isobel,' Jessie pleaded, frantically beating at the glass with both fists. Some powerful, inexplicable force was drawing her inside, despite her brave resistance. 'Let me go,' she shivered, hunching her shoulders and gripping the edges. A new surge of strength seemed to course through Jessie's veins. As if the frightful old hag realised it, she cursed and barred her teeth.

'Obey me, I command you,' she snarled. 'I am the mirror to the spirit. The ills which exist in all men are reflected in me. Do not be afraid.'

Jessie realised that her tormentor was growing weaker.

'Smash the mirror,' cried the younger voice, suddenly growing louder. 'Hurry whilst you can, for soon her power will return. Then we shall both be lost.'

'I'm sorry if I frightened you,' the old woman coaxed, her voice surprisingly sweet. Evidently she was changing her tune.

Jessie's heart thumped with anger and revulsion. Quickly, she twisted round, taking the full weight of the frame on her arm before hurtling it to the floor. There was a deafening crack. The mirror instantly shattered into a million pieces.

A rush of cold air knocked Jessie to her knees. When she came to her senses, Tommy was shaking her back to consciousness, his face ashen white.

13

THE CAMEO BROOCH

In the next week the snow began to melt, draining the streams and rivers and causing widespread flooding. Sheep were brought down from boggy pasture and cattle confined to sheds, where they were fed on winter silage. Jessie gloomily roamed around the farm-yard up to her ankles in mud, wondering if she had made a terrible mistake in releasing Isobel from the mirror. She could not tell anyone what had really happened in the shed, not even Tommy. Repeatedly, she relived the frightening episode in her mind.

After supper Jessie discovered Grandpa hunched over the kitchen table, having barely touched his food. His shoulder constantly bothered him, and the ligaments were proving slow to heal, in spite of his regular visits to the physiotherapist. It would be a long process, but a farmer couldn't afford to make an invalid of himself. Yet there was something troubling him even more.

He looked strained and worried as he examined the object resting in the palm of his hand, which on closer inspection turned out to be a cameo brooch. It was probably Victorian, but Jessie had never seen Gran wearing it.

'What's the matter, Grandpa?' she said, wondering why an attractive piece of jewellery should cause such concern. Jessie took the brooch, which was remarkably elaborate and quite beautiful. She turned it over, noticing the gold was tarnished and earth-stained. Nevertheless, a good clean would soon restore it.

Reflecting for a while, Jack Mottram remained silent. He was an independent man, sometimes stubbornly so, and found difficulty in sharing burdens. More than anything else, he wanted to protect Jessie and Gran, but everything had gone dreadfully wrong. The past would never allow him to forget, so it was pointless keeping up the pretence.

'Have you seen this brooch before?' he asked Jessie, his eyes narrowing suspiciously. His hand trembled.

She thought hard. There was something slightly familiar about it. But why was Grandpa so upset?

'I wouldn't be angry or anything,' he added, trying to encourage her.

Jessie's mind drew a blank. 'I can't remember having seen it,' she replied. Panic suddenly gripped her, and settled in the pit of her stomach. 'Is it a family heirloom?'

'Reckon you could call it that,' Grandpa said, in a tone which suggested that this was an unfortunate fact. Then he muttered something under his breath about bad luck and ill omens.

'But where did you get it?' she asked, unable to disguise her curiosity.

Grandpa held it up to the light, trying to jog her memory. 'I hoped you could help me with that,' he mumbled.

Why didn't he believe her? Articles which have been lost for years, sometimes just turn up, and Gran had recently tidied the attic.

Noticing her puzzled look, he continued in a quieter voice...

'It belonged to a lady, who died here a very long time ago,' he began, 'and I'm quite sure we don't want it at all. It was laying on the table - there; bold as brass.' He seemed angry now: his face reddened. 'I reckon it was just waiting to be found.'

This did seem incredible. Jessie braced herself. The horrible sick feeling came again. She swallowed hard. Then she remembered. Yes, she had seen the cameo brooch before - in the painting of Isobel Mottram, stored in the attic. She was quite sure. It was pinned to the neck of her velvet dress.

'What's wrong?' said Grandpa.

Jessie envisaged the old hag and shivered. It didn't make sense. Had it all been a fiendish plot? She wondered if the young

Isobel had tricked her; after all she and the old woman were one person. Mrs Drummond certainly had her doubts about Isobel. Now the words of the old lady came flooding back...

'They claimed she was a crazy woman and a witch, and there were some who would have burned her at the stake, had it been permitted. But it's true she dabbled in magic, believing she could outplay Beelzebub at his own game. That's where she came unstuck, I reckon.'

It was a terrifying thought. But if Isobel had escaped the evil that ensnared her, it was peculiar that she should remain to haunt them. Unless her business was not finished.

The phone rang and Grandpa went into the hall. Unable to face further questioning, Jessie rushed past him to her room. She hoped he had not discovered the smashed mirror, or she really would have some explaining to do.

That night she had a confusing dream. It had a lot to do with the discovery of the cameo brooch, and whether Isobel intended to harm them. She had gone to bed uneasy, pulling the blankets over her head, in an attempt to shut out the world. But there was nothing in the least bit frightening about the dream, which was unusual in itself, considering she was crossing the moor after darkness. In front of Jessie walked the small figure of Billy Mottram, carrying an oil lantern. Occasionally, the boy turned to summon her!

The apparition left a clear trail of footprints. These glistened black in the thin covering of snow, whilst there was no indication whatsoever of her own passing. She could see other tracks, such as those of foxes and rabbits, and the trail of a horse-drawn carriage, which had laboured over the hill. It was a kind of role reversal. Jessie had become the ghost, which would explain everything, including her own sense of detachment. The past was the present now.

In the crisp moonlight, the moor appeared even wilder; an endless expanse of whiteness without familiar landmarks. Jessie was thoroughly enjoying the adventure. Her limbs were light as air, and she felt absolute freedom from normal constraints. Movement was without physical effort, as she happily drifted across a rough cobbled road and through a jungle of thick prickly gorse, without a care in the world.

There was Billy, exactly the same distance away. Even though he didn't seem to be hurrying at all, it was still impossible to catch up with him. Eventually, they passed between the cleft of two hills, where the wind was bitter and moaned vocally, as if in a deep cavern. A wide stagnant swamp lay ahead, surrounded by stretches of saturated earth and black mosses. Billy looked up.

Somehow Jessie knew that here Isobel met her fate. Maybe Samuel Mottram chased her into the bog, or the Devil claimed her - as Elsie Drummond suggested. No one knew for sure. It seemed that Isobel Mottram had just vanished into thin air.

Next morning when Jessie dragged her aching limbs from bed, she noticed scratch marks and leech bites all over her legs and arms. It was horrifying. Had she really sleepwalked across the moor at dead of night, following after Billy? Quickly she pulled on trousers and a long sleeved shirt, and hurried downstairs.

It was nearly lunchtime. Gran was busy peeling potatoes.

'I thought I'd let you sleep,' she said, pouring a fresh cup of coffee. 'Why you look exhausted.'

Outside Joe and Sam were replacing rotten timber in the barn, which had come off badly in recent winds. The big oak by the gate had taken a severe battering. One branch was leaning dangerously. Grandpa insisted that they deal with it immediately.

Jessie spent the rest of the day digging out the brook, which was blocked and flooded. She enjoyed the work, apart from the occasional downpour which left her soaked to the skin. Lost in her own thoughts, she had almost reached the bridge before she sensed someone was watching her. From the corner of her eye she caught a glimpse of a solitary figure. Around her head, the wind was chanting in a voice which sounded human. Above, crows circled the muddy fields with loud raucous shrieks. A flock of nervous sheep scattered across the moor. The atmosphere was unnerving.

'Whose there?' Jessie called, forcing herself to look round.

Standing next to a tree was a tall man, wearing a riding cloak. He was watching her closely with a malicious look in his eye. Jessie froze. There was something unnatural and terrifying about him. She noticed the cruel twist of his mouth and arrogant stare, which was cold and repulsive. His face might once have been regarded as handsome; apart from the mottled pock-marked skin and the nasty festering scar above his eye. Then, in the time it took her to blink, he was gone, disappearing amongst the trees below the footpath.

A sickening smell of sulphur lingered in the wind. Where he had stood the ground was shrivelled and burned.

14

A PREMONITION

Ever since her frightening encounter with Samuel Mottram, Jessie was drawn ever closer to Billy. Frequently, she thought about him and her feelings of unease grew steadily stronger. Sometimes she dreamed. Dark empty dreams, where she was either trapped in a grey room with just one chink of light, or running across the moor pursued by a terrible evil. Occasionally she felt as if Billy's life was merging into her own.

Once in the shed she believed she caught a quick glimpse of him, although it was actually broad daylight, and the sun's rays through the damaged roof made vision hazy. Only Jessie couldn't be sure. The rescue of Isobel, she hoped would bring Billy back, but nothing had really changed - apart from the re-emergence of the 'shadowy things'. These were becoming fiercer and more dangerous. They boldly entered the farmhouse to plague her.

She could spot them crouched in dark corners; strange tricks of light at first glance, which caused her to doubt her own mind. Then they would grow, change shape and rearrange themselves as if they could read her vulnerabilities. Once they emerged as snarling black hounds, but mostly they were gnarled, elongated imitations of people, their fingers like waving tentacles from the sea. Nor were they silent: thin whispery voices rattled like dead leaves, and sometimes Jessie heard their demonic laughter and weird chanting. Mrs Drummond's grandmother had believed them to be malevolent spirits, who had relinquished their corrupted souls to the 'Dark One'.

Was Isobel Mottram amongst them?

Jessie tried not to think about it, especially since the occurrence of the footsteps, which no one but herself could hear. They were from the light tread of a riding boot. The wearer was most likely to be a woman. Jessie was convinced she was Isobel. The footsteps originated from exactly the same spot. Thirty-eight steps in all she climbed, which seemed remarkable, since there were only thirty-four at Boulder Tor Farm. Jessie counted them carefully, but the discrepancy was quickly resolved, when Gran explained that the staircase had been altered some forty years back, accounting for the four missing stairs.

The intruder passed across the corridor towards Billy's room, where the footsteps hurried, and a hand tapped several times on the door, with the hollow sound of a riding cane. Then slowly and deliberately she turned the handle. But the door always remained fully closed. To prove it, Jessie had tucked paper inside the frame. It was obvious that Billy never answered her entreaties. Could it be that Isobel remained evil?

Mrs Drummond seemed convinced of it.

She arrived early one Saturday morning to visit Gran, and to deliver an elaborately decorated cake intended for Jessie's birthday. The old lady looked pale and wore a hooded expression, suggesting something was eating away at her.

Gran appeared anxious, as she drew a comfortable armchair close to the fire.

'The hill is very steep and slippery, Elsie, and you shouldn't have come all this way on your own. Still, I'm delighted to see you.'

Mrs Drummond wrinkled her face. 'Oh, don't make such a fuss, Liz. A good walk never harmed anyone. Besides it's been a considerable time since I visited Boulder Tor Farm. I thought I'd like to see the old place again.'

Gran nodded, as if in mutual understanding. 'Yes, but you should have let me collect you, at least.'

'Nonsense! I'm not too old to make it on my own steam,' she faltered. 'Really, the truth is Liz - that I needed to talk to you.'

'What about, Elsie?' Gran swallowed.

'I know this must sound strange, but I've had a premonition of some kind.'

Jessie leaned closer to the doorframe, curiosity overcoming her dread of being caught listening. Gran sounded nervous, her voice wavering uncertainly.

'I hope it wasn't too terrible.'

Mrs Drummond grimaced. 'I'm afraid it was. And that's why I've come to warn you. It's young Jessie who I fear for most! I hope, with all my heart, that you will send her home.'

'Unfortunately, that's impossible at the moment,' Gran said. 'Her mum is abroad and won't be back until well into the New Year.'

'More's the pity. But there must be something we can do?' Elsie Drummond sat back in her chair and her mouth trembled slightly. 'Yesterday morning I supposedly collapsed, but of that I'm not altogether convinced.'

Gran let out a startled gasp. 'But shouldn't you be resting in bed now. What will your nephew say?'

It seemed likely that the old lady had suffered a minor stroke, and should be kept as calm as possible.

Elsie Drummond guessed Gran's thoughts, but dismissed the idea with a shrug. Her eyes glazed over as if she stared at some distant thing..

'It was like a horrible vivid dream at first,' she recalled, wringing her worn hands in despair. 'Yet, there was a remarkable reality, which left me in no doubt that I was wide awake - and witnessing a terrible injustice.'

Gran's face paled and her eyes stared out wildly. 'No, Elsie! It all happened a long time ago. Why should it start all over again?'

'Because the curse has come full-circle,' the old lady replied slowly. 'There is nothing you or I can do about it. I've seen the horseman, Liz. His laughter was enough to freeze the blood!'

Standing behind the door, Jessie trembled. She had also experienced the indescribable terror, and knew exactly how Mrs Drummond felt.'

Gran's face was a mask.

'Why do you not believe me?' the old lady scolded. 'And what indeed would account for all these burns?'

The injuries were deep and raw, quite similar to those inflicted on Jessie and Grandpa. But it all seemed so incredible. Elsie Drummond was evidently unwell.

'Let me at least offer you a drink,' Gran said.

'Jessie is in extreme danger,' repeated Mrs Drummond, waving her hand and declining the offer. She needs to go from here quickly. I witnessed something not yet happened, and believe folks can influence fate, if they know how.'

'But why Jessie?'

'Don't you see - your granddaughter is a catalyst. I'm not saying that the Mottram Curse wouldn't have eventually reached this point. It's obvious that it must be resolved in spite of everything. But she was meant to come here - fate dictated that. Unless we can think of some other course, it seems that Jessie must pay the price.'

'Oh, why did she have to open the locked door?' Gran moaned. 'And she smashed the dreadful mirror, Elsie, like I told you on the phone.'

Realising that her secrets had been discovered, Jessie recoiled. She strongly suspected that Grandpa knew too.

'I expect it wouldn't have made much difference,' sighed Mrs Drummond resignedly. 'She commanded her - the witch, I mean. At least the glass is shattered to pieces, otherwise things might have been a great deal worse.'

'You think?'

'I'm certain her power will be diminished. Isobel Mottram has the Devil's wiles; pretends to be one thing, when it's apparent she's another. Some folks believed she could change form: a gift from Beelzebub himself. After she disappeared into thin air, a great black beast was sighted prowling the moor, and the villagers blamed her for the slaying of their cattle.'

'Wasn't that a bit far fetched, Elsie?' Gran retorted. 'They believed all kinds of superstitious nonsense in those days.'

'Laugh if you like, but you've said yourself that she haunts you now.'

Gran averted her eyes from Mrs Drummond's stony gaze.

'Yes, I believe so. But I can detect no hint of malice in her presence. I actually saw her Elsie. She was standing over there by the clock, as clear as anything. She was no more than a girl, but her eyes were sad and sorrowful.'

'Only a ploy to win your trust,' Mrs Drummond scornfully replied. 'But you can't imagine what's lurking inside her mind, neither do you know whose side she's really on! Billy Mottram isn't so easily fooled.'

'What do you mean by that?'

The old lady paused to catch her breath. 'What the Devil wins the Devil keeps, or so the old saying goes. Isobel Mottram will never change her spots, so don't you go falling for her tricks.'

Mrs Drummond cast a disparaging glance at the cameo brooch worn about Gran's collar.

Jessie was surprised that Mrs Drummond was so set against Isobel. Nothing it appeared would convince her otherwise. But she was even more astonished that Gran had actually seen the ghost, and was wearing her cameo brooch. Was it something to do with Isobel's powers of persuasion?

Jessie returned to her room. After a while she heard Mrs Drummond's footsteps on the stairs. She headed down the corridor in the direction of Billy's room. For a moment Jessie was undecided whether or not to follow. Then she slipped out, only to find the old lady waiting for her.

'Jessie, dear, I wondered where you were.' There was a quizzical look on her face. 'I think we ought to take a look at Billy's room, you know. Something tells me he's in some kind of trouble!'

As the pair of them stepped through the doorway, Jessie reeled in shock. The walls of the room had turned a musty yellow again, and were mottled with stains and damp patches. Furniture was moved around. In the space normally occupied by a single wardrobe, was a stretch of dingy wall where a painting had once hung. It had been rectangular shaped with a wide frame, made clear by the discoloured plaster surrounding it.

For a brief moment the portrait of Isobel Mottram stared down from the wall, fiercely guarding the room.

Lost in confusion, Jessie hardly noticed Mrs Drummond trotting about in an agitated manner. She was scrutinizing the place with an astute eye.

'It appears that Billy hasn't been around for ages. Weeks I'd say.'

'What?' Jessie blinked.

'Billy,' repeated Elsie Drummond, in a loud voice. She paused as if testing the air. 'I'm afraid he's been driven out by something evil. He can't come back, you know - unless we rid the room of 'them'.'

'But who are they?' she asked.

Mrs Drummond caught her breath. 'No one is absolutely sure, but they've been around the moor for centuries. Evil spirits of some sort, I should imagine.'

'I've heard them whispering,' Jessie confided.

'Ah, and chanting, I expect. They're good at that! But they come from no holy order, of this I'm certain.'

The old lady began to unpack a sinister looking bag, containing a weird assortment of items. There were phials of curious smelling mixture, white dust, swollen roots and herbs and parched animal skins, along with a tattered old book full of unfamiliar signs and symbols.

'It's best if you don't witness this,' she said, nodding towards the door. 'The powers of evil are at their worst when challenged.'

'But...'

'Please do as I say,' she ordered.

Disappointed, Jessie closed the door behind her, just as Elsie Drummond lit the first candle.

15

ISOBEL'S PORTRAIT

After Elsie Drummond's visit, Gran watched anxiously over Jessie. At night she brought the dogs into the house and they slept in the hallway, alert to every sound and movement. But the farmhouse was much quieter now, although it was an empty silence, brooding and expectant. Grandpa sensed it too. He paced around or slept in the armchair, occasionally groaning in his sleep.

The 'shadowy things' had retreated, which was an overwhelming relief to Jessie. Sadly their withdrawal did not bring Billy back. His room remained much the same, although the smell of stale bog grew fainter. Gran had thrown open the window. The daytime brightness seemed to penetrate gloomy corners; all except for the spot where Isobel's painting had once hung. This seemed to retain a shadowy presence, which even the winter sunlight couldn't dispel.

Once Jessie thought she caught a quick glimpse of Isobel in the mirror beneath the stairs, and wondered if she dreamed it. Her lavender perfume wafted along corridors, and she discovered long red hair tangled in her hairbrush. Why was Isobel Mottram haunting her?

Jessie believed she knew.

After lunch was the time to act. By then Gran would be shopping in Plymouth, and Grandpa busy with Joe repairing fences in Fern Bank Field. She'd have to hurry though, since she promised to help Sam with the cattle feed at two thirty.

'Best get a move on,' Jessie encouraged herself, fearful that her courage might fail.

If everything went according to plan, the portrait of Isobel would soon be restored to its rightful place. Then Billy's mother might feel some degree of forgiveness.

Gran watched Jessie suspiciously. 'Are you really sure you don't want to come?' she said. 'We could do a bit of Christmas shopping together.'

She shook her head guiltily. She didn't want to let her grandmother down, but she had made a promise to Isobel. Eventually Gran set off, rather later than expected, and after a great deal of fussing, which wasn't like her.

'I've asked Sam to keep an eye on you,' she said, before reluctantly driving off down the narrow stretch of road.

When the noise of the car engine had receded into the distance, Jessie walked slowly back to the house. Did Gran suspect she was up to something? Shrugging aside her doubts, she collected the ladder from the shed. Next she found the big torch; the one which Grandpa said gave out the light of a million candles. She decided only to use it in an emergency, fearing that Billy's cat might be lurking about. A funny thing - she actually missed the animal. That done; she made her way purposefully towards the attic, only to find that the hatch was wedged closed, and took some considerable force to open.

Jessie's heart missed a beat.

As she entered the dark space again, she was hit by the same cold feeling. It seemed peculiar how this confined space felt so different from the rest of the house. Pigeons must have entered through a hole in the thatched roof. There was evidence of serious rain damage. She peered round, screwing up her eyes. Mottled light fell on the piles of junk and discarded furniture. The attic looked even more disorganised than usual. Jessie imagined she saw mocking faces in dark corners, but turned away, convinced that her mind was playing tricks on her.

Obviously someone had been up here again, probably Gran searching for something. Jessie guessed it was the Christmas tree which now stood in the hallway, all decorated with purple and silver baubles. She sighed with relief, until she noticed the disturbance in the far corner by the wardrobe, where she had first discovered the portrait of Isobel Mottram.

A mixture of panic and surprise struck Jessie, which she couldn't rightly explain. Maybe Gran had destroyed the painting on Elsie Drummond's advice. Anything was possible. Suddenly she felt choked and her throat was dry as dust. But Isobel's ghost had acquainted itself with Gran, so why would she wish to alienate it?

Uneasily, Jessie edged forward.

Eyes seemed to follow her from the shadows. She imagined the scowling face of a bearded old man, glaring down from the ceiling. Then the light changed again and the image was gone, turning itself into a flickering flame which Jessie thought looked like a candle.

Refusing to be intimidated, she stepped across the creaking floorboards, consciously gauging the distance between herself and the wardrobe. She was aware of a tight feeling in her chest and her breathing was rapid and shallow. Jessie knelt down to search the mouldy heaps of newspapers, until she located the painting hidden beneath. She ran her fingers along the cracked old frame, before pulling it out and inspecting the dark canvas.

It seemed a good deal cleaner. Someone had obviously been at work! Gran, she decided; probably inquisitive about the cameo brooch, which she wore in spite of Grandpa's protestations. Anyway, she was spared the task of removing cobwebs. Carefully she placed it on the chest of drawers.

The portrait had been damaged in several places, and then crudely restored. Someone had apparently taken the trouble, although it was unlikely to have been Gran or Grandpa. Grandpa, in particular would never have touched the painting. Even Jessie decided it was too dark for her tastes, although there was no denying the beauty of Isobel Mottram. It was easy to imagine she had been maligned by cruel rumour, for her face belied none of that evil of which she was accused. But the words of Elsie Drummond kept coming back to Jessie...

'What is attractive on the outside might be rotten within'.

Jessie did suffer misgivings. She questioned why Billy did not return, now that the 'shadowy things' had been banished from the house. Swallowing her doubts as best she could, she threw a tattered mildewed cloth over the painting, until nothing could be seen apart from the tarnished edges. Even so, she could feel the portrait staring at her, and a peculiar hypnotic calm ebbed through her veins. Her eyelids felt heavy, as she lifted it through the hatch.

What a dreadful fright poor Gran and Grandpa would have.

But Jessie's guilt was overshadowed by the urgent desire to bring the painting back to Billy's room. The need was so great, that she suspected Isobel Mottram was directing her.

Checking first that Grandpa and Sam were nowhere to be seen, she hurried towards the locked room. The door was slightly ajar, as if expecting her, and there was no need to use the key. She wondered if this was a positive sign. With hammer and picture hook retrieved from a hiding place in the wardrobe, Jessie began the task of reinstating the portrait, positioning it in the empty space on the wall. It looked perfect and seemed always to have hung there. A soft warm light glowed before her eyes, when she stretched up to touch the canvas. Isobel was smiling down from the portrait as if she was still alive.

There was no turning back now, whatever fate might hold in store. Jessie remembered what Mrs Drummond had told her...

'What began in the Mottram family must be finished there!'

The enormous burden weighed heavily on her. But supposing she failed and let everyone down. The idea was too horrible to contemplate. She visualised Billy running before the horseman, and his cruel murder in Postbridge Field. Not least of all she feared for Gran and Grandpa. She prayed with all her heart that Isobel was genuine.

Suddenly extreme cold struck Jessie. Ice particles covered her clothing. A biting north wind raked her hair, turning her tears to crystal.

'No, Isobel,' she sobbed, as the portrait slowly faded into hazy greyness.

Jessie closed her eyes, overwhelmed by the horrible feeling that her heart had frozen inside her body. Rain blew through the painting, stinging her face like acid. Isobel was gone.

In her place stood a grey soulless landscape, so devoid of natural life, that Jessie was convinced she was witnessing the World of the Dead. As she stared in bewilderment through the bleak window of the painting, and into another dimension, she knew that she must stand fast. Isobel wanted her to know the truth.

The scene might have come from her worst nightmare. Screaming inwardly Jessie sank to her knees, willing everything to disappear. But the sickle moon cast eerie rays on the bizarre spectacle beneath. There were seven sharp boulders forming a wide arc across the landscape. They were huge and pointed, and so covered in cracks and fissures that the wind moaned through them. Above these a terrible dark shadow reared upwards, quickly blotting out the moonlight. It was a colossal illusion against the night sky, and blacker than blackness itself. The 'beast' bore no resemblance to any living creature; a horned monstrosity which gave physical form to the vilest and most evil of thoughts.

Jessie averted her eyes and prayed.

When eventually she dared look up again the image was gone, lost amongst a terrifying avalanche of cloud, red as blood. In the cloud there were ugly demon faces, and funny bat-like creatures fluttering about. On every rock and ledge candles burned, illuminating the arrival of a ghostly audience.

They were Victorian lords and ladies, squires and landowners, all dressed resplendently in fine silk and satin. They didn't look incredibly evil, Jessie thought. Perhaps greed and vanity had been there undoing. Wigs adorned powdered faces, fingers glittered with gold and diamonds. Some wore lavish face-masks, like ghostly revellers of a long past ball.

Jessie knew that the apparitions were no longer human, and they could only materialize on unholy ground. Here dark forces were at their greatest, and the laws of evil had full reign. In this grey world, nothing living could survive for long. No doubt these cursed rocks had been used for sorcery, where the Devil's chosen ones had pledged their wretched souls.

Was Isobel Mottram warning her?

16

THE DEVIL'S TEETH

Jack Mottram picked listlessly at his food, his face streaked and blackened. His clothes reeked of charred straw. Every so often he coughed to rid himself of the overpowering stench which had settled on his lungs. Outside Hank and Tommy were still cleaning up. Overnight, the thatched roof of the farmhouse had been struck by a bolt of lightning. Large chunks of blackened straw were scattered across the yard, along with heaps of thatching, from where the roof had already been stripped for repair.

Gran was thankful the damage was no worse. That was down to Jessie! She had sounded the alarm.

Jessie wasn't quite certain what woke her. As she tossed and turned in her sleep, she experienced a heavy weight on her chest, making it difficult to breathe. Next she smelt smoke, and dashed barefooted and panic-stricken into Grandpa's room.

Now she grimaced, as she swallowed coffee. Her throat was sore and her eyes stung sharply. She wondered why Grandpa was glaring angrily. But he had snapped at everyone today, including Hank and Tommy, and moaned constantly that 'ill luck' would be the ruin of him.

'We should be real proud of Jessie,' said Gran, bemused.

'And that we will,' Grandpa hissed, 'when she learns to do as she is told.'

Jessie was startled. She had never seen him look so angry, but there was fear in his eyes too; real fear. The fire had begun directly over Billy's room and she wondered if that was frightening him, or had he already discovered the portrait of Isobel?

Gran levelled her gaze, and for the first time Jessie saw a hint of scorn in it. 'What's got into you, Jack Mottram?' she stormed. 'You've no right to talk to Jessie like that. This isn't her fault, you know.'

If Gran expected him to back off, then she was evidently mistaken. Grandpa looked more angry than before; his face contorted, as he slammed his fist hard on the table.

Jessie jumped up with surprise. She wondered if the Mottram Curse was actually driving him mad. He looked beside himself with fury. It was horrible to witness Gran and Grandpa fighting.

She had to stop it - somehow. 'I'm sorry...,' Jessie stammered. She felt guilty that she was the cause of their heated argument. 'What have I done?' she asked, realising she would have some explaining to do if he really had discovered the reinstated painting.

Grandpa leaned over towards her, until Jessie could feel his breath on her face. It was like someone had put an evil spell on him. This wasn't her Grandpa.

'Don't go near Elsie Drummond again, ever again,' he yelled, hardening to the old lady once more. Ever. Hear me?'

Gran slumped back in her seat in total amazement. 'What are you talking about, you fool, or have you gone completely mad? Elsie looked dreadfully ill, when she came here to visit me; and I have been worried about her ever since. I reckon she's had a stroke, and is in no state for any trouble from you.'

Grandpa looked unmoved. Jessie wondered why he was being so obnoxious.

'Then she had better leave us alone,' he shouted. 'So it's true, she's been here spreading her poison. She's a witch, I tell you; and a troublesome one. I don't want her putting crazy ideas into Jessie's head. We've got enough problems already.'

'We certainly have, ' Gran replied loftily, 'and we don't need any more from you.'

Jessie remembered the letter in her pocket. She hurried from the table, deciding to make herself scarce. The letter was neatly written and from Elsie Drummond, requesting that she visit her as soon as possible. There was a note of real urgency about it, and she wondered if Mrs Drummond was in some danger. No matter how much Grandpa ranted and raved, Jessie knew she must go.

Collecting her coat, she closed the door quietly and walked outside. The wind was sharp as a needle. As she passed the window, she noticed Grandpa slumped across the table, as if all the strength had drained from his body. Why did he hate the old lady so much? Hiding away from the real problem was what Grandpa was best at! Jessie wondered if he would ever understand Billy's terrible predicament.

She shivered visibly as she leaned on the gate. Cold seemed to pass through her body as if it was hollow. The tears that welled up in her eyes and streaked her face, Jessie wiped away with the back of her hand. Never had she felt so lost and vulnerable. Ashamed of her own weakness, she knew that Billy depended on her. From somewhere she must draw courage.

'Are you alright, Jess?'

She swung round, startled. It was Tommy Myers, with fragments of scorched thatching still stuck to his clothes. He smelled of charred straw, but it was still Tommy, and Jessie couldn't help but feel pleased to see him. He wiped a grubby hand on his trousers and walked over. Somehow, he always made her feel better.

Jessie dropped her head, and smiled through her tears. 'Why can't I ever do anything right?' she shrugged.

Tommy put his arm round her. 'Look it's not your fault; none of this. Just forget it happened. I heard your Grandpa's raised voice. He's lashing out because he's frightened. Like a fish caught on low tide, he doesn't know where to swim.'

Together they walked towards Fern Bank Field, where they sat on the hewn trunk of a two hundred year old sycamore. The hawthorn hedge was ablaze with seasonal berries. An icy calm hung over the moor, freezing their words in the stillness.

Suddenly she had to tell him about Isobel's portrait. Unable to keep her secret any longer, she felt compelled to share it with someone.

'I have done something really stupid,' she sighed, her voice sounding fast and breathless. 'I hung the painting of Isobel back in Billy's room.'

Tommy looked puzzled. 'What's wrong with that? Wasn't she Billy's mother?'

'Yes,' Jessie replied, miserably. 'Only, I don't know why I'm so afraid. I can only think that I've made a terrible mistake. Mrs Drummond says she's evil, but then Grandpa believes Elsie Drummond is a witch.'

Tommy wrinkled his brow and looked puzzled. 'Just slow down, Jess,' he said. 'Let's discuss this logically. Do you think Isobel is evil?'

Jessie gulped and felt guilty. It was as if the serene face of Isobel was looking at her now. 'I don't know,' she replied, her voice faltering as she recalled to Tommy the horrific scene she had witnessed through the painting. She described the seven sharp boulders, which arched across the soulless landscape. How the horned monstrosity had reared its hideous head into the night sky, and the ghostly audience had gathered on the rocks to worship.

Tommy listened attentively. His face paled and his body sagged. He didn't want to believe it, for Jessie's sake. If it was true, she had witnessed the Devil and his followers in the blackest part of the moor.

Then she turned towards him, looking into his eyes questioningly. 'You recognise that place don't you, Tommy? Where is it?' she demanded, growing even more agitated. 'I want to know.'

Tommy had never seen her like this before. Her mood was a mixture of terror and excitement. It scared him, and he wanted the familiar Jessie back.

He loosened the grip on her hand. 'It's called the 'Devil's Teeth he reluctantly replied. 'No one ever goes there - because the place is cursed. '

'You must take me!' Jessie said, urging him to his feet with a sudden jerk. Her voice rang out with determination.

'This isn't a good idea, Jess!'

Jessie's voice suddenly dropped to a whisper. 'I've got to see it for myself,' she said. 'That way I'll know what's best to do.'

Tommy led the way across the moor, until they reached a narrow track. Dappled shadows from the watery sun seemed to stalk them. They stepped across slippery moss- covered stones and through a clearing flanked by skeletal trees, which creaked and groaned in the winter wind. There were only streams and gullies for landmarks.

Eventually Tommy pointed towards a passageway between two towering rocks. Jessie was surprised to find that the journey had taken less than half an hour.

Before long the 'Devil's Teeth' rose up before them - a colossal monument to evil. There stood the seven boulders, enormous and pointed, and the wind moaned eerily through them, as if they had living breath. Below, Jessie recognised the rocky outcrop where she had witnessed the ghostly revellers. A gnawing sickness ate away at her stomach, as unseen eyes watched them from shadows.

Here stood a place of grey lifeless evil, unchanged in a million years, where death had snuffed out life, mocked and imitated it. It was a void, which answered to no natural laws.

Tommy saw the figure first and instinctively drew back, pulling Jessie into a rocky crevice overshadowed by a wide ledge.

There, standing in a hollow was a hunched, hooded shape, no more than five feet high. It was slight in stature, and almost swamped by a monk-like habit. Amongst crags, the wind whined eerily.

Tommy and Jessie crept forward, hardly daring to breath. The coarse grass was stiffened with hoar-frost and the silence frozen. Small dots of light were beginning to appear. These burnt with a bluish tinge, and flickered confusingly before their eyes as they edged closer.

The figure was busily lighting candles in a circle, whilst chanting in a horribly dry voice. The language they did not understand, but Jessie could discern vibrations in the earth, deep and rhythmic. She began to feel sleepy.

Then it lifted withered hands up to the sky, and a winged shadow appeared from above.

'We shouldn't be seeing this,' Tommy whispered. 'Cover your eyes, Jess.'

But Jessie was compelled to watch, as the ring of light intensified in heat and burned a livid orange.

The figure knelt down, rather stiffly, and began to draw signs and symbols in the dust, obviously copied from a thick volume laying close by. Suddenly, as it raised its stick-like arms, the ring slid upwards, now rocking and shimmering in the night sky. For a few brief seconds it just hung there quivering, until it completely disintegrated into a core of black ash.

'Come on,' Tommy whispered, covering his mouth to prevent himself coughing. Dust had settled on his lungs and it was difficult to breathe. To his horror, the sorcerer looked directly towards them, but luckily turned away unseeing.

Jessie hesitated. 'Wait a minute,' she replied, as she witnessed the frail figure pick up its bags and shuffle down the track, all strength deserting it.

'No, we don't,' Tommy gasped, tugging roughly at her sleeve. 'We're going home, right now.'

But Jessie wore her determined look. She had to know the truth - who this person really was? Otherwise she was behaving like her Grandpa. Something told her that the figure was clearly no ghost or 'shadowy thing'. It was a real person, and one in possession of formidable power.

It seemed like tempting fate to Tommy. Luckily they had escaped. Following the hooded figure might only invite more trouble, but he had to protect Jessie. Sometimes she could be so foolhardy, he could hardly believe it.

A faded sun peered through saggy clouds, as they set out across the moor again. This time Jessie led the way, always keeping a safe distance from the stooped figure. Her heart beat in her chest with a dull methodical thud. Her mouth was dry with fear, although she didn't care to admit it. Occasionally, the figure stopped to draw breath, and she and Tommy took cover behind the rocks. Eventually quickening pace, it turned towards the road about a mile past Boulder Tor Farm.

There it progressed to the gate of Ivy Cottage; where the cowl slipped from its face to reveal the true identity.

To Jessie's disbelief and utter amazement - the sorcerer was none other than Elsie Drummond herself.

17

MRS DRUMMOND'S CONFESSION

All night long Jessie tossed restlessly, and wondered if Grandpa was right about Elsie Drummond. When she finally fell asleep, she experienced a warm peaceful feeling as though the old lady, was watching over her like guardian angel. Eventually Jessie awoke with a start. Hoofs thundered on stone and the loud whinnying of a horse shattered the silence. Below in the yard Meg was barking a noisy greeting, as Jack Mottram returned from his early morning ride.

Jessie sighed. Grandpa was pretending again. He was pretending everything was fine and the Mottram Curse just didn't exist, when all the time it was growing ever closer. Otherwise, why would he go out riding alone after his terrible accident? Soon the curse would come full circle. There would be nothing he, or anyone else could do - unless its terrible challenge was met.

Jessie quickly scribbled a note in her diary. *It read - 'tomorrow is Christmas Eve and my birthday. Have visited Billy's room most days, but still no sign of him. Wonder what Isobel is up to!'*

Pulling the hairbrush through her blonde hair, she rushed downstairs. Jessie gave a quick glance at Grandpa's muddy riding boots, left tidily at the door. Gran usually scolded him, if he wore them inside the house. Just now, she looked too busy to notice.

Thankfully everything seemed perfectly normal, and Jessie realised how jumpy she had become. Piled high on the Welsh dresser were her birthday presents and cards. She felt guilty that her friends had remembered her, when she had become so absorbed in the Mottram Curse, that she had barely given them a second thought. There was a parcel from New York sent by her mother, next to a neatly wrapped gift from Tommy. But how could she celebrate her birthday, when it was on that fateful day that Billy Mottram was murdered?

Grandpa was carrying on as usual. 'Don't look so down in the mouth, Jessie,' he grinned. He motioned to Gran. 'We've invited lots of folks round to celebrate Christmas Eve. We're gonna have a real good time.'

Jessie couldn't help but smile to herself. It was so easy to guess the reason.

Gran and Grandpa didn't want to be alone at Boulder Tor Farm. They were like two children, afraid of the dark. Did they really believe it would make a difference? Jessie had witnessed how quickly time and place could change. It was a predicament where normal rules didn't apply, and a battle must be fought in the empty void; where odds were hopelessly stacked against the living. Only Elsie Drummond might be able to help them.

Witch, or no witch, she was in possession of remarkable powers. Jessie knew she had to trust her. As soon as the opportunity arose, she would visit the old lady without preconceptions, without judgement and willingly take any help she could offer. But it was going to prove more difficult than she imagined.

Grandpa seemed to be keeping a constant watch. Gran set Jessie numerous chores, including cooking and preparing food for the guests. When at last she had completed these, Grandpa presented her with a huge basket of holly and a silver spray can, and asked her to make even more Christmas decorations. She even considered an unexpected bout of sickness, but decided that was unlikely to work either.

'Help me please,' she muttered desperately. Then, as if in answer to her pleas the doorbell rang, and Jessie heard the voices of Fred Goodridge and his wife.

What a stroke of good luck. That meant they would be

preoccupied, and she could plan her escape. Wasting no more time, she took a basket from a peg in the kitchen and headed towards the back door, patting Meg to silence her loud barks. She would gather up a few cones and holly sprigs to explain her absence.

Today the lane reflected an eerie silence. A low wind rattled through bare beech trees, and their branches swayed like giant arms. Jessie followed the slippery muddy track through open fields, the icy wind whipping her face and freezing her cheeks. She scrambled over a gate, towards the lane which led to Elsie Drummond's cottage.

A Christmas tree was prominent in the front window. In the tall fir tree close to the conservatory hung an assortment of colourful lights, which were no doubt the handiwork of her nephew.

'Nice, aren't they?' Mrs Drummond called out, popping her head round the door.

Jessie almost jumped out of her skin.

'Sorry if I frightened you,' she smiled. 'I've made some coffee. Come quickly inside now, you look quite frozen.'

Jessie hesitated, before walking slowly towards Mrs Drummond's front door.

There was something different about her today. Her cheeks looked hollow and she had aged considerably, but never before did her eyes shine with such light and energy. The old lady put her hand on Jessie's arm.

'I've got so much to tell you, my dear,' she said. 'I've been waiting for you to come.'

She led Jessie through the hallway, and into the front room with its large bay window. Jessie stared round. She had never seen this room before. It was dark and old fashioned, with a dreary pink settee and armchairs. By the wall stood a heavy oak table, etched with strange signs and symbols; as were thirteen chairs, all with uncomfortable looking backs, where those seated would have to sit bolt upright. On a shelf close to the open coal fire stood a magnificent crystal ball, which reflected through its faceted surface, a multitude of glittering colours.

Mrs Drummond settled in a comfortable rocking chair, whilst Jessie wandered around the room looking at everything. There were tarot cards, spell books, bottles of herbs and potions. A cast iron cauldron with one broken leg, was balanced precariously on the 'Encyclopaedia of Witchcraft'.

Mrs Drummond chuckled to herself. 'I only keep that old thing for a bit of fun,' she said, looking amused.

'My Grandpa believes you are a witch,' replied Jessie.

'Then your Grandpa is right. I am a witch - a white witch, and will never deny it. So was my grandmother before me. But that is of no concern. Unlike my grandmother, my power has always been very weak, although when I was younger folks believed me to be a 'medium'.

'Medium?' Jessie repeated.

'Yes,' replied Mrs Drummond. 'People who are able to contact those on the other side.'

'And could you?'

Elsie Drummond winced, as though she did not like to be reminded. 'I shall only speak the truth to you, Jessie. No! I only pretended I could. People wanted to believe, and maybe I took advantage of them a little bit.'

Jessie steadied herself. She was glad she had sat down, because now her legs felt weak and shaky.

'Regrettably, I was a charlatan,' admitted Mrs Drummond, until a few months ago, that is. Then something quite extraordinary happened.'

The room seemed to darken considerably, as the old lady leaned forward towards Jessie. 'I began to have visions at first,' she murmured, wrinkling her hands nervously. 'Horrible visions. They were so real; it was as if I had been transported back in time. I saw the horseman and witnessed Billy's terrible fate. It was much worse than I imagined. Samuel Mottram set the moor alight, like I said, and Billy was burned as well as trampled in Postbridge Field. I can still hear him screaming. But that's not the worst of it.'

Elsie Drummond's face had turned a ghastly white, and blue thread-like veins stood out in her forehead. She looked so fragile and transparent, that Jessie just wanted to hug her. Instead she knelt by her feet.

The old lady took her hand. 'The Devil has returned to the moor - to collect his dues, I should imagine. He appeared above the 'Devil's Teeth' at dark fall, where the malevolent forces of the moor are gathering. They are preparing to claim Billy's soul, and yours also Jessie, unless we can think of some way to prevent them.'

Jessie shivered. There was no other solution. She must pass through the forbidden door in Billy's room precisely at the right moment, then into the grey lifeless world she had witnessed. A world where nightmares walked, and the living could only survive for a limited time. Most likely she would never return. Her heart went cold.

Mrs Drummond's face clouded in realisation. 'You've seen the World of the Dead, haven't you?' she whispered in a shaky voice.

Jessie nodded, expecting recriminations. She explained her dilemma over Isobel's portrait. How it had changed before her eyes. But Elsie Drummond only smiled, as if it confirmed something she already knew.

'You were so right about Isobel.' she replied softly, 'and I was well off target. Somehow I got it into my head that evil could never reform itself - but just goes on for ever, increasing in its own vile strength. Well, there you are. I was wrong, and not too proud to admit it. The things I said about Isobel were a grave misjudgement. Every sinner can repent.'

Jessie thought for a moment, 'But are you certain that she is repentant?'

'Totally convinced of it,' Elsie Drummond beamed. She drew her head close to Jessie. 'I have a confession to make. I've managed to communicate with both Isobel and Billy, she proudly confided. It seems so sudden, that after all these years of 'pretending', that I have become a 'real medium' at last. I feel a little bit frightened.'

'What did they have to say?' Jessie could hardly contain her curiosity.

Mrs Drummond drew a sharp breath. Even though she looked exhausted, her eyes gleamed with excitement.

'Isobel thanked you for trusting her. It was your trust that set her free! It warmed her soul, and gave her the courage to overcome the 'corrupt power' which had imprisoned her all those many years.'

'But why did evil imprison her?' Jessie asked cautiously.

Mrs Drummond let out a loud sigh. 'In later life, Isobel Mottram played a very dangerous game, I'm afraid. She tried to challenge the 'Dark One' in the hope of rescuing Billy's soul, but everything went dreadfully wrong.'

A cold chill settled on the room. Through the misty window snow whirled in a thick cloud.

Jessie's mind raced. 'Was Isobel a powerful sorceress?' she replied.

'Very powerful!' exclaimed Elsie Drummond. 'And thankfully, she has learned from her mistakes.'

'Mistakes?' Jessie puzzled.

'Yes! The Devil's path is through Samuel Mottram. Destroy him and the route is finally blocked. The Devil would have no passage, and he cannot intervene, so the Mottram Curse would be broken forever. Sounds easy, doesn't it?' she laughed grimly. 'But of course, it isn't.'

'Samuel Mottram only survives on fear,' Jessie added, measuring her words carefully. 'Fear fuels the demon - didn't you once say that? Without it, he is nothing.'

The old lady nodded with understanding. 'No more than hoofs on a windy night,' she agreed. 'Billy could have rid himself of his ghastly nightmare, if only he had overcome his terror. But that is easier said than done, we both know.'

'What does Billy say?' Jessie replied, anxiously searching the old lady's face. 'You spoke to Billy too.'

'Ah, and so I did,' she sighed, her face suddenly darkening. 'The worst of it, is that now Billy is resigned to his own fate. He says he loves you, and above everything else, does not wish to endanger your soul.'

'But I'm in terrible danger already,' she gulped. 'If the

Mottram Curse is allowed to take its course, then surely all of us will be destroyed. Doesn't Billy knows that? I must go to find him through the forbidden door.'

'It seems so,' sighed Mrs Drummond, resigned at last and very sadly. Remember I will assist you to my final breath. There are other forces to protect you too - powerful ones. These will act as your guides. Give it your heart, Jessie, for I sincerely believe given the right circumstances, evil can be defeated.'

The snow was falling heavily, as Elsie Drummond showed her to the front door. Already the garden was covered. Jessie raced through the gate and down the slippery lane, breathing the fresh crisp air.

'Hurry straight home,' the old lady called after her. She turned and waved.

The snow came right up to Jessie's ankles. Huge flakes fluttered past her face like white moths. She pulled up her hood. The light was quickly fading into misty greyness. An icy wind froze her lungs and occasionally she looked round, but nothing followed save a boisterous wind. Breathless and cold, she reached the gate of Boulder Tor Farm, where Hank Myer's truck was still in the driveway.

She instinctively looked up.

In the window of the locked room, a pale candle burned. It was no more than a weak flicker of light, so fragile that the slightest breath of wind would extinguish it.

Jessie smiled. Billy had come home at last.

18

DARKNESS BEYOND

Jessie woke at half light, when she heard a dull monotonous thudding like a hammer striking snow. It sounded again in a rolling wave that hurt her eardrums. Reluctantly she got out of bed, hardly daring to guess at what it might be. Hesitant at first, she moved towards the window, her face fixed in an expression of dread.

Hardly conscious of her own actions, she wiped away the condensation with her bare hand. Jessie blinked nervously, as flickering images confused her eyes. At first she could make out nothing, only a white expanse of blankness met her vision, until she noticed to her horror that a wide band of snow was actually moving. It was motoring along at a terrific pace, as though a vast snake was wreathing and twisting beneath its surface.

She drew a sharp involuntary breath. This wasn't possible. It shouldn't be happening. Jessie hid her face in her hands. When she dared to look up again, the vision was so close that she could clearly see the churned up snow on either side. More terrifying still was the thunder of wild hooves, as an invisible rider veered nearer, before galloping across the open moor.

Dawn held back and never seemed to break, until finally it appeared over the hill, grey and mottled like a withered leaf. Grandpa was already in the yard, muffled up to his ears and ready to feed the cattle. He stamped the snow from his boots, and listened to the restless commotion of the animals. Meg crouched at his heels. A shed door banged loudly and Grandpa jumped. Jessie knew he had plenty reason to be nervous.

Quickly she dressed, then found a woolly scarf and gloves

in the drawer. She couldn't leave poor Grandpa on his own. He looked so frail and vulnerable. She took a thick windcheater from the wardrobe, and in the pocket deposited the key to the locked door. The door wasn't locked anymore, but that didn't matter! The key had come to represent the close bond between Billy and herself. Somehow Jessie sensed that was the most important thing of all.

A few minutes later she was running after Grandpa, her boots crunching through the brittle snow. He was already in the Long Barn, back turned.

Straw crackled; a beam creaked. Stamping cows moved backwards and forwards in their stalls. Every sound was unusually loud and for a moment she hesitated, feeling puzzled. She could smell hay, silage, sweat and urine, and the hot steamy breath of the cattle, their tongues lolling over troughs of grain. It was an overpowering combination, which made her feel dizzy and disorientated.

Startled, Grandpa swung round. 'Oh, it's you lass!' he exclaimed, in a relieved tone. Don't creep up on me like that.'

Creep up on him. Jessie could have laughed out loud. A herd of stampeding elephants would have made less noise. Surely there was something wrong here. Grandpa's voice seemed extremely loud.

'Take no notice of me,' he said, pretending to be jolly. He put his arm round her, his mouth still fixed and tense. 'I'm just a bad tempered old fool,' he groaned, realising how he must sound. Fear could make monsters of folk, causing them to rant and rave at loved ones.

But it was the feeling of helplessness. It seemed as if he was trapped down a deep, dark well and could never get out. Jessie was such a clever girl, much older than her years, he thought. How he wished he could do something to protect her. It was her birthday today. What must she think of him?

Jessie sensed his despair and her heart melted. 'Grandpa,' she whispered, giving him a big hug. 'What's wrong?'

Even her whisper sounded extremely loud. She realised her senses must have been heightened.

'Nothing we can't handle, love,' he replied. 'And Happy Birthday.'

Jessie sighed out loud. Grandpa wasn't going to share his fears with anyone. It was obvious that he had withdrawn right into himself again. Resigned, she pulled a sack of feed from the rack. They worked silently, side by side for a while.

'Where's Gran?' she asked, still aware of the loud pitch of her voice, which had started to irritate her. Gran was usually up before anyone else, but there was no sign of her this morning.

Grandpa didn't answer straight away. His eyes looked dim and distant. 'Oh, you know your Gran,' he said at last. 'Likes to make herself useful, she does. Well, some neighbour has gone down real sick,' he continued, 'and what with the snow and everythin', Gran thought she should go off and nurse her.'

Jessie puzzled. 'What neighbour?' There weren't many neighbours around, the farm being quite isolated.

Grandpa coughed. 'Er... some poor old girl,' he replied, as if he didn't mean it! He waved his hand dismissively. 'She'll be back soon enough. Gran wouldn't miss your birthday for the world.'

That was the end of it as far as Grandpa was concerned. But at least Gran was safe. No dreadful accidents or anything like that. Jessie thought, well aware that Christmas Eve wasn't the best time for the Mottrams.

Soon afterwards when Grandpa and Jessie went inside, they were met by the delicious smell of cooking. Bacon, eggs and fried bread sizzled in the pan. Hank Myers was busily frying, and Tommy gave Jessie a cheeky grin as he set the breakfast table. She was glad he had stayed over. Jessie needed Tommy more than ever now.

Grandpa stared vacantly through the window at the world outside. It seemed like he wasn't part of it now, but he still worried over Gran. Snow whirled in a great blizzard, blown by an icy cold wind. The moor was covered over in arctic whiteness, and every scent, noise and colour was temporarily suspended. It seemed unlikely that any of the Christmas Eve visitors would arrive tonight, and most had cancelled already.

Grandpa suddenly shivered.

'Don't care for the weather much,' Hank said, as they settled for breakfast.

Jessie decided against opening her birthday presents until Gran arrived home. The truth was that she felt less than enthusiastic on this dreadful day. In spite of everything, it was cosy in the kitchen, with the heavy oak table close to the open fire. Soon, she felt a peculiar strangeness. A kind of vivid awareness, where ordinary objects were pronounced and well defined. Curtains rustled, china tinkled, and from somewhere came the distinct sound of a wind-chime. It had an eerie quality, which made Jessie feel very uneasy.

Whatever was happening to her?

The scene around her was growing more unreal. Even Grandpa, Hank and Tommy, were becoming shadowy figures in the back of her mind, their voices disjointed and unfamiliar. Jessie was struck by a sudden isolation, as if she did not belong here at all. Panic rose up in her throat and threatened to choke her. Swiftly she ran from the table, past the pile of birthday presents and the Christmas tree in the hallway, and then into the yard outside.

There the extreme cold hit her like a sledgehammer, along with the indescribable loneliness. It was a distant, remote feeling; as though she was the only living person in the world. Terrified, she looked round.

The snow was gone, but a thick frost had now settled on the cobbled yard. Beneath Billy's window a huge oak tree swayed noiselessly. An ancient plough stood close to the old fashioned gates, knotted with ivy. Above the glistening, white-roofed barn, a ghostly owl glided, casting its eerie shadow on the stones beneath. Night hung dark and heavy, but a tiny light still burned in Billy's room.

Jessie knew that she must fulfill her promise to help him. Ideas only flitted through her head, but made no sense. Doubts crossed her mind as if to hinder her. Did she really possess the power to change fate; to turn time backwards and recreate the past? It did seem quite incredible. But most important of all,

Billy seemed to believe in her.

All noise had died. Jessie was disturbed by the absolute silence. Somehow, it throbbed in her ears, so she couldn't be totally deaf. Yet there were no obvious sounds, not even a creaking bough or rustling leaf. The heavy, now unfamiliar door of Boulder Crag Farm was opening, and she walked towards it with a heavy heart.

The past was coming back to haunt her.

The hall looked quite different, but still came as a shock to Jessie. In place of Gran's gilt-edged mirror hung an eerie painting. Stuffed birds and animals in dusty glass cases peered from every corner, and beneath a stained-glass window (which definitely hadn't existed before), stood an antique spinning wheel. It was identical to the one in the shed, which Gran and Grandpa had argued about. Jessie shivered as she ran past the frame, which began to tremble and vibrate as if some invisible hand was hard at work. The test of her courage had begun.

But where was Billy? Jessie turned in time to catch sight of a fleeting shadow on the wall. It moved steadily on four legs, its tail upright. Once or twice it stopped, as if to wait for her. The shadow of the cat moved with feline grace, and it was difficult to keep up. Eventually they passed together through the wall of Billy's room. It seemed a natural thing to do.

Jessie was overcome by a sense of detachment. Her limbs felt wonderfully light. It was similar to floating on air; her natural inhibitions muted. Hurriedly she followed the cat's shadow, not able to think of anything better.

The room was bathed in dingy yellow light, as though viewed from a dirty window. Over everything hung a misty wet vapour. Jessie winced at the atmosphere of neglect. An icy chill carried the breath of the marsh, and a mirage of endless moorland filled the tiny space. Wanly the moon shone through faded curtains. The stench of stagnant bog permeated every corner. Isobel's portrait was surrounded by an eerie glow.

Colourless eyes fixed on her. Jessie froze. The shadow of the ghostly cat crouched at her feet in warning.

Suddenly she could hear the crashing hoofs again, followed by Billy's screams of terror. Every nerve in her body began to tingle. Fear had returned and the horror of being pursued. She looked round, but nothing was there. Nothing but the inexplicable terror she had experienced in Postbridge Field, when Billy's consciousness had impinged upon her own.

'Billy,' she whispered soundlessly. Her lips were ghostly white.

The low grey door was slowly opening.

19

THROUGH THE DOOR

As Jessie approached the door, her skin began to crawl and every fibre of her body stiffened. She peered down through the dark whirling mass of movement. It was like a black hole in space, opening up to swallow her. But she had to go through the door - had to find Billy and save him. She was his last chance. Drawing a deep breath, Jessie stood on the threshold, the shadow of the cat still by her side. The darkness seemed to reach out, as if it had been waiting.

Down, down into the void she went.

Her screams were silent. Air raced through Jessie's lungs in a rush, but it was too thick and heavy to be real. She could feel it through her fingers. Nothing surprised her here; gravity followed unnatural laws. It hurled her through space at colossal speed. It was impossible not to be afraid. Her heart pumped with such a ferocious rhythm until she feared it would stop altogether.

Samuel Mottram was laughing. 'Go away,' she shrieked, kicking and lashing out frantically. Suddenly Jessie was aware of the freezing cold, stinging her back to consciousness. Had it all been a terrible dream? There were no footsteps in the glistening snow where she had woken. Her head throbbed painfully. Confused and disorientated, she scrambled to her feet.

The moon appeared full and round, bathing the ground in icy blue light. Seven sharp pointed boulders formed an arc across the landscape, identical to the scene from Isobel's painting. Staring up at the huge crags bowing above her, Jessie could again sense the inherent evil of the place. Dark forces dominated every stone and grain of earth. It belonged to the devil - just as Mrs Drummond believed. Here his wicked followers had flocked and sworn allegiance to evil. Screaming inwardly, Jessie sank to her knees. It was a horrible feeling, as warmth suddenly evaporated from her body. Tears blurred her vision, but instinctively she could see everything around, even the hollow where Elsie Drummond performed her incredible magic. She wondered about the winged shadow which the old lady had conjured, and hoped it would protect her now.

Low echoing vibrations sounded as through water. Jessie could hear again. She closed her eyes and when she opened them, eerie figures were standing on the ridge. They were tall, thin and colourless, with tiny dots of light for eyes. The 'shadowy things' were blind, but could detect the slightest movement. It was useless trying to hide. Already their elongated limbs were pointing and signalling to one another.

Jessie reeled in shock.

Frightful howling filled the frozen air. Electric fear coursed through her veins. The shadowy things were changing. They had become ferocious hounds, circling and baying for blood. They seemed real enough. The pungent scent of animal hung over them. Jessie could smell their musty breath.

The woods were still and quiet, registering every turn of her frantic passing. Twigs snapped, branches creaked and the crashing of her trainers sounded unreal. A light sprinkling of snow lay on the hills, and the wind stung without mercy. Jessie breathed deeply, filling her lungs with fresh air. Somehow, she managed to pace herself and as if by a miracle, remain just ahead of the snapping jaws.

But where could the living hide in the World of the Dead?

The moon waned, disguising its brightness behind black clouds. A velvety richness invaded the moor. Out of the trees now, Jessie could spot will-o'-the-wisp lights floating eerily, and low rolling thunder sounded across the hills.

Ahead of her stood the Ten Commandments Stone below Buckland Beacon, and to the left Bagley Woods. Jessie ran on, hurtling over rocks as if by instinct, the terrible hounds still on her trail. The ground ahead was spongy and waterlogged, so that her feet began to sink. The hounds were nearing, but why did they not bring her down? She could almost smell their hunger.

On the highest point of the Ten Commandments Stone stood a winged figure. Jessie looked up, her eyes suddenly drawn to the spot. She had a beautiful face and was surrounded by an arc of vivid blue light. The figure was Isobel Mottram.

Then the hounds were gone and Jessie was free to run again. She was Jessie once more, her long hair flying behind as she raced down the hill. A great surge of energy coursed though her veins. The cold wind gave her new life. Now she could think clearly again. It seemed strange to be so close to home and still a century away. Even more peculiar was the fact that Gran and Grandpa hadn't even been born. They had inherited the vengeful curse through no fault of their own.

Fine snow hung on the wind and trees merged in grey confusion. Jessie focused her eyes on the dense tunnel of undergrowth, conscious of the growing tightness in her throat.

The flapping of an alarmed bird reverberated, its panicked shriek sounding long afterwards. She had no idea how she could run so far. But something else bothered her! The air was different. It had become acrid and difficult to breathe, so quickly she buried her face in a handkerchief and hurried down the hill. Desperate thoughts of Billy filled her mind. He was here somewhere, she could sense his head-numbing terror, causing her nerve ends to tingle. Gradually her entire body shook, as Billy began screaming inside her head. It was absolutely unbearable, the strangling terror inside her chest as if her lungs had been turned inside out.

Billy Mottram was choking.

Beyond the sky was a mass of billowing smoke and blackness. Wind buffeted blazing trees and drove smoke through tangled hedgerows. There stood Boulder Crag Farm as it had looked a century ago, and now amidst a sea of advancing flames. This was no ordinary fire. It tore through snow and ice with furnace heat. As Jessie cleared the final hollow, the agonised cries of Billy thundered through her mind.

What was happening? She threw herself down, rolling in

the powdery snow and furiously beating at her own body. The pain was excruciating, although she wasn't actually on fire. It was the most cruel thing imaginable.

Billy Mottram was burning.

Jessie could feel the terrible flames scorching his flesh; hear his agonized cries of torment. As Elsie Drummond described, Samuel Mottram had torched the boy in Postbridge Field. She shivered as she recalled the horseman; the hot sulphurous smell and the weird choking in her throat. She had survived because Billy rescued her. Now, she understood his torment. If fear had created the monster then she must destroy it.

Whatever, she had to save Billy Mottram. Determined, she headed off towards Postbridge Field.

An orange fireball hovered above. The heat was so intense that Jessie was forced to shield her eyes. Vision was distorted and hazy, as sharp pains stabbed at her pupils. A vast pillar of smoke billowed upwards, obscuring the moon and every single star. Struggling to keep the balance of her mind, Jessie knew there was no turning back now, neither for herself nor Billy. She hesitated, her lungs crushed by a sudden rush of air. The black cat, no longer a shadow, ran by her side.

Billy was here, trapped in a fiery tunnel, and already the rearing vision of the horseman was upon him. Red mist surrounded the fearful apparition, which was horribly disfigured. But worst of all were his eyes, which glowed malevolently and reflected all the ills of the world. Even so, Jessie could not look away. She moved towards him, without any will to stop herself.

Desperately she clung to Mrs Drummond's Saint Christopher pendant. Somehow she had to break free from the spell of the rider, as Jessie dodged and weaved to avoid the lurching horse. Blinding sparks stung her face. The vile stench of steamy breath almost suffocated her. A crushing weight settled on Jessie's heart. It was too late.

Billy's fear of his uncle crossed the very boundaries of terror, and it was this, and nothing else that was fuelling the demon. What made her believe she could resolve the Mottram Curse single handedly? Hearing the triumphant shriek of the horseman, Jessie stumbled. Everything was lost, as he read her tortured thoughts. The apparition was growing even stronger now. The distorted face had become a skull. Grotesque, shrivelled hands were reaching out. Jessie could feel herself lifted bodily on to the horse's back. She wriggled and squirmed as bony fingers tore at her. In the struggle the key to the locked room tumbled to the floor, but she hardly noticed.

'Billy,' she mumbled through ashen lips.

The horror of Jessie's plight had finally reached him. The boy began to stir. He moved steadily, crawling forward on hands and knees; a small waif-like figure against the vast shadow of evil. The indescribable terror once etched on his face had gone, replaced by a terrible anger. His small hand reached out for the chipped black key.

Jessie shuddered at the sharpened blood-stained dagger, no more than a centimetre from her throat. One slight movement and everything was lost. The breath stopped in her throat. Confused she stared at Billy. What was he doing?

Samuel Mottram seemed oblivious. Never in his wildest dreams did he envisage Billy ever escaping from his prison. Fear locked the door on him a century ago! That fear was everlasting, and the Mottram Curse would exact its final vengeance.

Billy hurled the key into his uncle's face.

Vivid orange flames leapt before Jessie's eyes. She was no longer on the horse's back, but crouched amongst swirling dust and ashes. There was no sign of Samuel Mottram, or his demon horse. A warm breeze blew. The smoke had cleared, as though blown away by some unexplained force. In the ebony darkness, a startling bright light had arisen. The light revealed the smiling faces of Billy and Isobel.

Someone else was moving down the path, picking her way through rocks at remarkable speed. She strained her eyes. The figure was old and bent, but walked with surprising agility.

Overjoyed, Jessie threw herself into the arms of Elsie Drummond.

20

SAFE AT LAST

Laying back on her pillow, Jessie wondered if Gran and Grandpa could ever really understand what happened to her. She doubted it. There were some things she was not entirely sure about herself. How had she arrived back at Boulder Tor Farm after Elsie Drummond waved goodbye?

But she was certain that Billy was safe at last. The challenge had been met and the Mottram Curse gone for ever. Now Samuel Mottram was nothing more than dust and ashes. When she recalled how close to annihilation she had come, Jessie shivered. Billy saved her soul, when it was meant to be the other way round. Nevertheless, it was the sheer horror of her own predicament which had prompted his actions, enabling him to overcome the terror of his uncle.

A remarkable peace settled on Jessie, so that she was content to drift in pleasant oblivion, rather than recall the terrifying events of Christmas Eve. When she woke up, there was Grandpa sitting by her bed looking pale and tired, having suffered a rough night. But the fear in his eyes was gone, now that the spell of the curse was broken. Gently he leant towards her.

'You've been right poorly, Jess,' he said, worry still clouding his face. 'Given Gran and me a proper fright.'

It wasn't until a couple of days later that she was allowed downstairs, when the worst of her fever had past. Everything seemed remarkably normal. Gran was busying herself preparing lunch. A blazing fire burnt in the hearth, where Grandpa relaxed in his comfortable armchair with Meg at his feet.

Jessie screwed up her eyes. In the flickering flame, she imagined the smiling face of her father. Something told her that he too had been released from the horrifying curse. But she still felt confused. The entire episode was like a jig-saw puzzle with the last vital pieces missing.

'Now don't you go fretting,' Grandpa said, noticing her puzzled expression.

'Tommy found you,' interrupted Gran, 'and not a moment too soon. He went off searching with Meg in Pudsham Wood, though I haven't the slightest clue why you should be there.' She smiled. Deep lines and furrows seemed to have left her face. 'But it was just as well he did. You weren't even wearing a coat. Heaven forbid what might have happened.'

'But Mrs Drummond kept me safe,' Jessie explained. 'She brought me down from the high rocks. I was completely lost and wouldn't have made it without her.'

She recalled how relieved she had felt to see a familiar face, and couldn't wait to discuss everything with the old lady. 'Maybe I should phone now…'

Gran and Grandpa exchanged perplexed glances.

Gran coughed nervously. 'I'm afraid that won't be possible, Jessie,' she replied very sadly. 'Elsie passed away in the early hours of Christmas Eve. I couldn't tell you, especially on your birthday. But she died very peacefully in her sleep.'

Mrs Drummond was the neighbour whom Gran had rushed off to nurse. Tears stung Jessie's eyes. Why hadn't she realised? She remembered how Elsie had scaled high rocks with ease, and moved swiftly down mountain tracks. The old lady had been a ghost herself.

'Well, stranger things have happened!' Grandpa exclaimed. 'If you say Mrs Drummond helped you, then we've got no reason to doubt your word. We'll go lay flowers on her grave tomorrow, and say thank you.'

Gran nodded and put her arms round Jessie.

In the following weeks, there was an atmosphere of peace and contentment at Boulder Tor Farm. Even the shadow of Billy's room was gone for ever. Gran decorated and furnished it to match the rest of the house, although the portrait of Isobel Mottram still remained in place. Grandpa never voiced any objection. He also had been hard at work. The shed was almost empty now - Jessie couldn't resist having one last peep. The remains of the frightful mirror had disappeared, along with the rest of the junk. A strong smell of saddle soap permeated from orderly piles of tack, as Sam looked up from his labours and grinned.

When wandering across the moor together, Jessie and Tommy found that many of the 'black spots' had lost their menacing atmosphere. The 'shadowy things' were gone, and a restful quiet settled on the 'Devil's Teeth'. Even Postbridge Field was totally different now. The grass was cut and all evidence of the haunted barn removed. Sheep grazed there contentedly, hardly bothering to look up.

The Mottram Curse might never have existed.

Jessie felt inside her pocket. In a small tin lay the blackened key to the locked door. She found it on the rear steps of the farmhouse late one night, although how it came to be there - she couldn't guess!

.